John Riley's Daughter

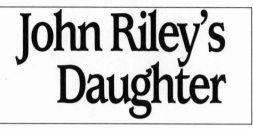

John Riley's Daughter

Kezi Matthews

Pedro Menendez
H. S. Media Center

42915

FRONT STREET / CRICKET BOOKS
CHICAGO

For Cardell,
whose unwavering friendship
graces my life

I wish to thank
my editor, John D. Allen,
for his skill, insight, and support.

Copyright © 2000 by Kezi Matthews
All rights reserved
Printed in the United States of America
Designed by Debra M. Porter
Second printing, 2001

Library of Congress Cataloging-in-Publication Data
Matthews, Kezi.
John Riley's daughter / Kezi Matthews.— 1st ed.
p. cm.
Summary: Suspected of having caused her retarded aunt to walk away
from their home in a small southern town in 1973, thirteen-year-old
Memphis must deal with her past and her future.
ISBN 0-8126-2775-X
[1. Family problems—Ficton. 2. Missing persons—Fiction.] I. Title.
PZ7.M43365 Jo 2000
[Fic]—dc21   99–058255

*And where is the place
of understanding?*
—Job 28:12

John Riley's Daughter

1

The summer I turned thirteen, "Tie a Yellow Ribbon Round the Ole Oak Tree" was all over the radio, President Nixon was up to his ears in Watergate, and my messed-up aunt, Clover Martin, disappeared off Blue Parrot Road in the middle of the day.

Saying you wish you could take things back is a big waste of time, because what's done is done. But I do wish I could take some things back—like the words I hurled at her that July morning in 1973.

"You crazy, hateful thing!" I screamed with all my might, racing to catch up with her. "I wish you were dead!"

The screen door slammed behind her like a slap in my face. The anger crashing around in my head goaded me to follow her out onto the porch, but she turned suddenly and looked at me with that strange light in her eyes. I backed off, my breath stacking up in my throat.

"My guitar!" she yelled. "Mine!" Her stiff, misshapen words flew at me on a thick spray of saliva. Then she turned and stomped down the steps. She was twenty-nine years old, but small and angular as a child. I watched her march across the yard and out of sight down the road, the tail of her ratty old coonskin cap flipping around as though it was still alive.

Her spittle clung like snail spoor to the outside of the screen. A fly circled the wet strings, then took off as I began to beat against the doorframe with my fist. This time she'd gone too far—way too far.

Aunt Birdie's old Buick cut sharply off the road and nosed up the driveway. She hopped out and hustled across the front yard, heading straight for the porch.

"My God, Memphis," she hollered, "can't Naomi leave for ten minutes without you two going at it like devil dogs? I could hear you clear down to my place!"

Birdie wasn't really my aunt. She'd been my grandmother Naomi's best friend since they were born, and she lived down the road from us.

The rage inside me began to flatten out as Birdie moved from the white glare of the sun into the deep, spreading shade of the live oak. The same old tune was headed my way. I'd heard it all before, over and over for the past five years. She cared about me, I knew, maybe the only one in Blue Parrot who did, other than my one true friend, Samson.

"Come on out here," she said, easing herself onto the swing at the shady end of the porch. She eyed me, dabbing at the perspiration on her face and neck with one of the big cotton handkerchiefs she carried around in the summertime.

I pushed the screen open, stepped out, and leaned against the worn doorframe. The morning heat was full of the relentless whining of the insects that flitted from the parched shrubbery to the porch and back again. I wouldn't look at her. I knew she had that certain little smile perched on her lips, waiting to soften me up.

"Let's see how those shorts fit," she said.

She'd bought a pair of patriotic red-white-and-blue shorts for me in Oaklee the week before. They were bunchy and too wide and made my legs look skinny.

"Cute," she said. "That top's just right, too." It was a star-sprinkled halter gathered in the front—the closest I'd come yet to a bra. "Looks like you're finally sprouting little tittie buds."

I rolled my eyes.

"You're all mottled up like you're fixing to cry."

I shook my head.

She sighed. "This day's a humdinger. Must be ninety degrees already."

She had an easy way of grabbing hold of loose ends and rolling conversations along without a hitch. She reached over and fished a sheet of newspaper from the wood box by the swing and folded it down to make a fan. Every time she swished it past her face, it made small snapping noises, and its breeze lifted her wispy blond bangs off her forehead.

"What was it this time?" She tilted her head and gave the swing a little backward push with her toe tips.

"She broke Rosie's guitar." The words felt as if they stuck to my teeth.

"The guitar? I thought that was locked up in the attic."

"I sneaked it out last year."

She looked surprised. "After all the ruckus it caused? I'm surprised Naomi let you keep it."

"She didn't. I hid it."

"And Clover found it . . . good Lord."

"She smashed it. The neck . . . right in two . . . on purpose." I crimped my mouth tight to hold back a sob.

Aunt Birdie rested the newspaper fan on her lap and studied my face. "Honest to God, Memphis, you look like you've been in a brawl."

I crossed to the steps and sat down, wrapping my arms around my knees. I knew Clover was broken inside her head, and after every awful fight I always had these good intentions—telling myself to let things slide, not flare up so fast. But that was easier said than done, and this time it was different. It was more than a smashed guitar. And I couldn't tell anyone, not Aunt Birdie, not even Samson.

"You've been doing this fandango long enough to know all the signs, honey."

"It's so unfair. Why can't Naomi just once—"

"Memphis?" She cut me off. "You just turned thirteen, right?"

Her birthday present—the bunchy shorts—was proof of that.

"It's a hard age, isn't it? Not little anymore, not quite grown." She started fanning herself again, the newspaper crackling louder at every flick of her wrist. "But seems to me thirteen's old enough to be taking some things in stride."

Aunt Birdie was always offering me a snack tray of reasons why Naomi was the way she was and why I had to learn to live with it. But after five years I knew what I knew, and one of these days, just like my mother, Rosie, I'd take off and never look back. I laid my cheek against my knees and closed my eyes.

"Can you imagine what it must be like living inside Clover's head?" The question sat between us like a rock. I knew it all by heart. Clover and the meningitis. Clover only two years old and in a coma. Clover messed up for life.

"That's not my fault." I said it just loud enough for her to hear and I could feel her staring at me. I was supposed to be ashamed for being so heartless. But I wasn't.

"If your mama hadn't lost her childhood playing second fiddle to Clover, who knows how all this might've turned out? Maybe she wouldn't have run off. Maybe . . ."

"Maybe I wouldn't have been born. And maybe it'll rain tomorrow. And maybe it won't." I was being hateful and knew it. I heard her gasp. "Well, isn't that what it always boils down to, Aunt Birdie? Clover does another shitty thing, and I wind up getting blasted for being John Riley's daughter. Right?"

"Don't go all stiff-necked on me, young lady. I don't know squat about your daddy—and I certainly don't blame you for the failings of your parents."

But she did know that Naomi was never going to forgive John Riley for his many sins against her—she'd heard it often enough. How he'd had Rosie cremated like a dead dog. How he'd dumped me and the urn with Rosie's ashes on her front porch and never looked back. It was Naomi's favorite thing to talk about whenever she'd had too much blackberry wine, and she didn't care whether I heard her or not. Sometimes it seemed she was waiting for me to jump to his defense. But I never did.

John Riley was a New York boy, out of an orphanage. Rosie and I were the only family he'd ever had, and maybe he had no idea what a daddy should be like. Maybe he'd just tried to figure it out as he went along.

I raised my head and looked over at Aunt Birdie. "He never would've left me here if he'd known it was going to be like this," I said. When she didn't answer, I added, "I think I would know whether John Riley loves me or not. And he does."

She smiled at me as if that was O.K. with her, but I could tell she was just going along. It didn't matter. One of the things I liked best about Aunt Birdie was the way she listened. And I never heard one peep back of anything I ever told her.

She stood up, smoothing out the creases of her sundress. Splotched red flowers exploded all over it, as though somebody had used it for rotten-tomato target practice. I pushed the thought away. There wasn't a soul in Blue Parrot who didn't like Birdie McCoy.

"Why don't you bring the guitar pieces over tomorrow morning? Next time I go to Oaklee, I'll see if old Grover can't do something with it."

I didn't answer, and she screwed up her mouth in a funny, deliberate way that showed off her deep dimples.

"When Clover gets back, honey, just go on about your business, O.K.? Don't be so quick to jump. You understand? If it starts up again, come on down to the house. You can always help me with the canning!" She chuckled at her own teasing and scrunched her fingers lightly atop my head as she went down the steps.

Right after my mother died, I used to dream of her every night. The dreams stopped when I went to live with

Naomi and Clover. Rosie just disappeared, as though she didn't want to be back in that house. I started to lose track of what she really looked like. Her guitar comforted me, layered as it was with memories of her fingerprints and the warmth of her belly. I dragged it around Naomi's house for weeks, anxiously protecting it from Clover's prying, pulling fingers. But I soon learned that once Clover got something stuck in her mind, she was like a freight train, throttle wide open. When our running battle turned into a shoving match, Naomi took the guitar away from both of us and locked it in the attic.

"It wouldn't hurt you to let her have it once in a while," Naomi said to me when she came back down. Under her breath she mumbled, "I should just burn the damn thing."

Four years later, right after my twelfth birthday, I had a dream about the guitar, that I needed to keep it in my room. I faked a stomachache the next Sunday, and after Naomi and Clover went off to church with Aunt Birdie, I got the keys off the nail behind the pantry door and climbed the narrow stairway to the attic.

Inside, the heat was bloated with the gloomy smell of mothballs, and within minutes I was dripping wet. Stringy ravels of dust hung from the rafters and trailed after me as I eased around the lumps and shapes crouching under yellowed sheets. Peering into the shadowy corners, I could make out huge cobwebs speckled with dead flies and dried-up insect pieces. I thought I heard little clickety feet scurrying across the floor.

I stood on top of a dilapidated leather-and-wood trunk and let my eyes slowly touch everything round the room.

Then the oak tree branch outside swayed, its leaves parting, and bright shreds of sunlight spilled through the dusty window. In that instant, a flicker of light danced off metal, and I saw the guitar's tuning head sticking out from behind an old pinewood dresser. I scrambled toward it, and when I touched it, my fingertips tingled. I hugged it close all the way down the back stairs and hid it under my bed.

One night soon after, I opened my eyes wide from a deep sleep and heard the guitar vibrating, calling to me. I got down on my knees beside the bed and pulled it out. Instantly I felt Rosie all around me, light as a hummingbird stirring up the air, smelling of orange sticks and incense. In the far corner of the room, a pinpoint of light began to grow, rounding, filling with a million dancing flecks of gold. From a place deep inside my head, I heard Rosie whisper, *Together—forever.*

I don't remember going back to bed. In the morning I wondered if it had all been a dream. Anyway, it didn't happen again, even when I tried to make it. But after that, if I woke up during the night, I could hear the guitar humming softly, telling me I wasn't alone. My mother's message was clear—as long as I kept the guitar safe, she'd always be nearby, and John Riley would someday find his way back to us.

After Aunt Birdie left, I went around the side of the house to the vegetable garden, wondering how I was going to explain this latest battle to Naomi—that is, if I got a chance to say anything before her temper blew. In less than a heartbeat, Clover had destroyed something I couldn't even put a name to and left me at the mercy of my tangled grief. I wanted to go upstairs to the guitar. I wanted to gather it up and hold it and beg Rosie not to leave me again. But the ache inside was too wild, and I had to break it down the only way I knew—by jabbing and slashing at the dogged, enduring weeds.

2

The first time Clover saw Rosie's guitar, some spirit deep inside her must have sensed its connection to her dead sister. It was a matter of seniority with Clover, I guess—Rosie had been hers long before she was mine.

John Riley left me on Naomi's porch in 1968, along with a cardboard carton filled with the remains of my life—mostly outgrown clothes, coloring books, the troll dolls Rosie loved to surprise me with, and her ashes sealed in a brown-painted metal urn. Right after she died, he said that she would want me to have her guitar. But he almost changed his mind as he stepped from Naomi's porch to leave. I could see it in his eyes. He caught my puzzled look, though, and left the guitar resting atop the carton.

We'd driven all the way up from New Orleans, and along the way he kept telling me how life was full of challenges and adventures, how proud he was to have such a stand-up, brave girl for his daughter. He said we were going to visit Rosie's mama in South Carolina. For my eighth birthday the day before, we stopped at a roadside stand and bought two big, juicy peaches for five cents each.

When we turned off the main highway at a sign reading "Blue Parrot, Pop. 900," he started getting fidgety and slowed our old green VW bus down to a crawl. He pulled into the first driveway we came to. It led up to a faded blue two-story house with a sloping tin roof, set back in the shade of an enormous live oak tree.

It was July, and what knotty patches of grass there were in the yard had already gone yellow. A wide, weathered porch ran across the front of the house and seemed to barely tolerate the dusty clay pots of wilting begonias clumped by the screen door. Tiny bursts of flame-red roses crowded up the gnarled wisteria vines at each end of the porch and spread across the front eaves.

Then I saw it. "Look, John Riley, they've got a swing!"

"How 'bout that!" His smile faltered. He drove the bus all the way up the hard-packed dirt driveway and circled back around the big oak so that we faced the road. Then he cut the engine, and we sat waiting.

"There's somebody at that window." I pointed up just as the curtain settled back against the screen.

John Riley lurched against the steering wheel as though his stomach had caved in, and I thought for a minute he was going to puke.

I don't remember Naomi saying much as we stood on her front porch and John Riley cried softly and talked me into her life.

"I'll be back just as quick as I can, baby girl," he said, squatting down to hug me. Then he stood up, took out his tattered wallet, and pushed a crumple of money into Naomi's apron pocket. "I'll send more soon." His voice cracked.

Naomi stood trancelike as he hurried to the old bus and jumped inside. When the engine kicked over and roared, she jerked forward and ran out into the middle of the yard, flapping her arms.

"Wait!" she hollered. "You can't just run off like this!"

But he did, giving me a frazzled smile and a thumbs up.

I wasn't concerned. I'd seen him go before, and he'd always come back. John Riley was a folk singer and had taught Rosie how to play guitar. She didn't like leaving me alone in the bus whenever they had a gig at a roadhouse or club, so I often stayed with one of their friends, old or new. John Riley told me he'd be back quick as he could, so I sat down on the steps to wait for him.

Naomi stood in the middle of the yard for a long time after he left, her arms wrapped tightly around herself as she stared up the road after the bus. Then she turned and looked at me, flinching as though her thoughts had restless little claws on them.

The screen door behind me creaked and slapped shut. I turned and saw Clover for the first time. The pounding of my heart roared up in my ears like the wheels of a big truck burning up highway. She was almost Rosie—same curly brown hair, same pretty doll face. Except the eyes were different, gray-green like Rosie's but distant and wary. And there was no smile.

I looked away, confused. When I looked again, she was sitting in the swing at the shadowy end of the porch, watching me, her small feet barely touching the worn boards. I jumped up and grabbed the guitar, which was almost as tall as I was. I ducked my head under its shoulder strap and started strumming. I only knew three chords, but it was enough for any song I wanted to sing. I ripped up the air with "You Are My Sunshine," cutting my eyes from one face to the other. It had always worked before, making people laugh and cuddle me. But Naomi and Clover just stared. The harder I tried, the worse it got. Finally I sat back on the step. In seconds Clover was hovering over the guitar that I'd laid next to me, her fingers plucking at its strings. I reached around and pulled it away from her.

"Might as well come on inside," Naomi said, heading toward me.

I smiled up at her, but she glanced away and went through the door. Clover, at her heels, threw a lingering look back at the guitar.

I figured I'd better stay put on the steps so John Riley wouldn't miss the house. I pretended to read the Little Lulu book that he'd thought hard about paying forty-nine cents for at a drug store just outside New Orleans. At the sound of every approaching car, my eyes darted to the road. Each one slowed in front of the house. The strangers inside would lean toward the open windows and stare at me before the car picked up speed and went on by. Every now and then I glanced at the screen door behind me, but no one was ever there. After a while I got hungry and finished off what was left of my box of animal crackers.

The sun turned a deep orange and slid down through the darkening purple-streaked sky to the horizon. I watched the first fireflies flicker up out of the rose vines, and the thin, metallic chirping of crickets lulled me into a limp serenity. It was getting late—John Riley would be coming back soon. I fought to stay awake as my eyelids began to sting and flutter. Just before I drifted off, I thought I saw a boy with straight black hair sitting in the shadowy bushes across the driveway, watching me.

In the morning I awoke in a strange bed. I'd been undressed down to my panties, and a small fan was droning atop a dresser in the corner. I sat up and looked around the room. My cardboard carton was sitting by the window, and Rosie's guitar was propped against the arm of a small wooden rocker. I listened for sounds in the house, but it was quiet. The sun was just rising. I slipped from the bed and padded over to the window. Off to one side, a pale ghost moon still lingered in the delicate pink sky.

I crept downstairs and found my way along the dim hall to the living room. The latch on the heavy front door flipped open easily.

John Riley's bus wasn't in the driveway. I pressed my face against the screen, willing him to appear, sure that he would.

I ran away four or five times the first month I was there. I never got very far up the road before Naomi's old blue Falcon would pull up alongside me and she'd throw open the door. "Get in," she'd say, and we'd ride in silence back to her house.

The last time, I made it up to the main highway and even thought I saw our old VW racketing up the road and disappearing over a hump. When the Falcon eased up behind me, Naomi cut the engine and got out. She folded down on her knees in front of me and grabbed my balled-up fists in her hands.

"Look at me," she said.

I stared down at the fading smiley faces Rosie had painted on the toes of my sneakers.

She tipped my face toward her. "Look at me."

I wouldn't.

"Listen, girl! You can come with me and make the best of it, or you can keep on walking up that road, hoping to catch up with that bastard, John Riley." She stood up, slapped the dust off the knees of her cotton slacks, and headed back to the car.

I looked up the highway. The bus was nowhere in sight. The Falcon's motor hacked a couple of times, turned over, and caught. I looked back at Naomi's freckled face behind the dingy windshield. She was staring straight at me, her eyebrows raised in little arcs.

In that moment, I understood in the harshest part of my brain that John Riley hadn't lost his way back to me. He wasn't driving up and down the highway, waiting for me to make my escape. I walked back and got into Naomi's car and I didn't try to run away again. But in my heart I knew that John Riley had made a terrible mistake. When he realized it, he'd come back for me.

The fight with Clover had eaten up the morning. Now the noon sun sat fierce and white straight overhead. I hurried around the side of the house, grabbed an empty peach basket and the rake and hoe from the back porch, and squashed on my straw hat.

The vegetable garden spread row after row across the backyard, fronting the chicken run. I worked off the raw edges of my grief-laced anger in the first hour. Then the weeding became the tiresome job it always was. I wanted to get it done before Naomi returned.

When Clover didn't come back after a while, I figured she must've gone down to the general store. Sometimes Mr. Johnson would let her sweep up and then give her a dollar and a sack of hard candy that she always brought home and hid in the back of the refrigerator.

I'd just hosed off the rake and hoe and was fixing to do the same to myself when the Falcon pulled up in the driveway. Naomi had been over to Oaklee on business about her widow's pension from the railroad.

She paused on the back steps, looked out across the garden, and nodded her approval. The screen door slapped behind her, and she called out to Clover. A few seconds later, she stuck her head out the door.

"Where's Clover?"

I shrugged, lifting my face into the stream of water. If she wasn't still at the general store, she was probably hiding inside the house, sitting stiff as a board at the back of a closet or in a ball under her bed, waiting for Naomi to find her with a great, heaving sigh of relief. It's what she always did when she wanted Naomi to know I'd been *bad* to her, that whatever fight we'd had wasn't her fault.

"Come on out," Naomi would coax. "It's all right. Mama's not mad." And that would be that.

Naomi's eyebrows drew together in a V. "Stop wasting that water," she said. "How long have you been out here?"

"Since about eleven."

"My God! It's four-thirty . . . and you haven't seen her since *eleven?*"

The screen door slapped shut again, and I heard her moving quickly through the house, doors opening and closing. She was checking all of Clover's favorite hiding places. As I reached for the door, she pushed it open.

"Her cap is gone."

"She wore it down to the store, like she always does."

"And you haven't seen her since?" Her exasperation was like a finger of blame jabbed in my face.

She phoned Aunt Birdie, who was at her side in minutes, patting her on the shoulder.

"Calm down, Naomi. Did you call the store?" She stepped back while Naomi reached for the wall phone next to the refrigerator.

Their eyes locked in a steady gaze as Naomi repeated the conversation on the other end. No, said Mr. Johnson, he hadn't seen Clover all day. . . . No, Georgene didn't see or hear anything. She'd been at the dentist all morning and was still all doped up, but he'd ask her when she came round.

"Call Gina," ordered Aunt Birdie, and Naomi dialed.

No, Naomi relayed. Mrs. Greeley hadn't seen Clover pass by. . . . No, old Hank had been sprawled on the back porch all day. . . . Yes, she'd look out back again and make sure.

"That's funny," said Naomi as she hung up. "Hank always follows Clover down to the store." The grizzled old dog liked Clover, though I never saw her say one word to him. He'd just fall in behind her. He'd sit and wait outside the store, then walk back up with her, peeling off at the Greeleys' yard.

"Maybe we'd better drive into town and ask around," Aunt Birdie said.

I jumped off the steps as they pushed outside and ran for the Falcon.

Naomi drove up and down the road two or three times, leaning out the window, calling at the top of her lungs, "Clover! It's Mama. Can you hear me?"

I ran around to the big live oak at the side of the house and scrambled up so I could see what was going on. The Falcon was kicking up a cloud of dust and gravel. Naomi just missed sideswiping old Hank, who'd ambled out to the road to see what all the racket was about. Aunt Birdie was hunkered down clutching the dashboard as the car swayed back and forth, roaring toward town.

What do I do now? I wondered. Before this day was over, Naomi would know that I'd stolen my own guitar and caused another big stink. I decided to beat Clover to the punch. I'd bring the mangled guitar down to the kitchen myself and just own up. I'd take Naomi's outrage on the chin without one whimper. That would count for something, wouldn't it?

3

When Naomi and Aunt Birdie weren't back by six o'clock, I fixed myself a tuna sandwich and sat out on the back steps to eat. All day my mind had flipped back relentlessly to the awful picture of Clover holding the guitar by its neck, her eyes locked in a burning stare. Over and over I watched myself frantically try to stop her, then freeze in shock as she raised it over her head and swung it down against the edge of the dresser with such force my old trolls jumped and skittered to the floor. I half expected to see blood oozing from the guitar's broken neck.

I choked down my food and wondered what it felt like to go crazy. Not like Clover's messed-up wiring, but really crazy. Round the bend, dingbat crazy. Sometimes I felt as though something inside my brain was eating me alive. I wanted to jump in front of Naomi and scream, "What about me? What about my feelings?"

Everybody in Blue Parrot knew Clover had a *history*. When she was about eighteen and the prettiest girl around, one of Swansons' kin passed through, looking to get on at the mill over at Oaklee. He spotted her at the general store and sweet-talked her into going for a ride in his pickup. When she didn't come back home on time, Naomi had half the town beating the bushes. Old Hallie Benson, out for her three o'clock walk down to the cemetery to visit with her dead husband, found Clover crying on the stone bench under General Beauregard's Oak. She walked her to Harrel's Drug Store and called Naomi. Though no harm was done, that boy had to make a run for it. Eventually it became a joke: one less Swanson over at the mill.

"Hey, Memphis."

I looked up as Samson came along the blackberry bushes at the side of the yard. We were the same age, but he wasn't growing as fast as I was, and he still had a kid's chunkiness about him, while I was all elbows and knobby knees. Aunt Birdie said, "Watch out. One of these days you'll turn around, and Samson'll be a foot taller than you. Take a look at his daddy, for goodness sake." He was sure enough an offbeat combination of his parents, with his daddy's clear blue eyes and slow smile and his mama's black hair and olive complexion.

Albert Greeley was a big, burly Korean War veteran with streaky blond hair and one leg shot off, though that didn't keep him from running Greeley's Auto Repair. Samson's mama, Gina, was an Italian woman from New Jersey, and they say it took her a long time to fit in when she showed up in Blue Parrot as Mr. Greeley's bride. But after a while, folks said Gina Greeley had a heart big as the sunrise, and her genuine Italian sauce made the church's annual October spaghetti dinner the talk of the county. Samson was the sun and the moon to his parents.

"Hey, Samson," I said.

He plopped down beside me.

"Wanna bite?" I stuck out the sandwich.

"Naw. What's all the ruckus about Clover?"

"She didn't come back from the store this morning."

"Y'all have another fight?"

"What else?" I'd never told Samson about the guitar and its mysterious power and I couldn't do it now without getting croaky in the throat.

"Maybe she got hurt or something."

"Well, wouldn't someone have called?" I flared up at him, not wanting to hear about how sorry we all might have to feel for Clover.

"Yeah, I reckon." He shrugged his shoulders and smiled at me.

"You know what she did last year?" I gave him a quick look, knowing he'd take the bait.

"Got in another car?"

"Uh-uh. Naomi was down at the church, sorting out rummage-sale stuff, and when she got home, Clover was nowhere around. Naomi was just getting ready to go hollering for her, when here comes Clover across the road from the field there. You'll never guess what she had in her hands."

His eyes widened.

"A bunch of baby mice, weeny little things, pink naked, with their eyes still closed."

"Naw!"

"She wanted to keep them in a shoebox up in her room."

"What happened to them?"

"You don't want to know," I said. Truth was, I wasn't sure what had happened to them, but I had a pretty good idea. In the morning, when Clover saw the empty shoebox and asked about them, Naomi said their mama had come for them during the night.

"That's the dangdest thing," said Samson. I could tell by the stricken look on his face he was thinking hard about the mice.

"Know what?" I bumbled on, trying to be funny. "She's probably over in that field right now, looking for another batch. Clover Martin, mouse kidnapper!" I threw back my head and pretended to laugh, but Samson just cleared his throat softly and went on feeling sorry for those baby mice. We sat there like two lumps, not speaking for the longest time.

Finally I said, "I heard Sonny Rayburn got caught stealing a Baby Ruth from the Dixie Mart."

"Yeah?" Samson eased a small, shimmery beetle off the bottom step with the toe of his sneaker, then reached over and set it right side up. "I never cared much for Baby Ruths myself." Then he added in that way of his, "Anyway, Rayburns don't hardly have two dimes to rub together."

They were dirt poor, that was for sure. Everybody knew old man Rayburn was an out-and-out weasel, spending what little money he had at the roadhouse.

"Oh well," I said, "they didn't do anything to him. Mrs. Benson stepped up and paid for it."

"Yeah, that sounds just like her."

We fell quiet again.

"Hey," I said, "I saw some stuff in the back of a magazine that'll slick hair down. Wonder if it'll work for me."

"Nothing wrong with your hair."

I snorted and bumped him with my shoulder. My hair's always been freaky, sticking out every which way at the slightest breeze and the devil to get a comb through. I cut it short in a fit of agitation one time, but it buzzed out like a porcupine, and I spent most of that year hiding the mess under an old felt hat I found in the hall closet. When it finally grew out, I settled on a ponytail down the back and let it go at that. I used to hate the color, too, until one afternoon Samson said every time he ate carrots, he thought of my crazy hair. I stayed awake a long time that night trying to figure out what he meant—and wondering just how often he ate carrots.

"If I was you, I'd leave my hair alone," he said, not looking at me.

I smiled—a little smugly—flipping my crazy carrot ponytail over my shoulder.

The setting sun dipped down behind the stand of pines on the hill, making it glow like a fairy-tale forest. We watched streaks of lavender and gold and smoky blue spread like melted jewels across the sky.

"I bet you could write a poem about something like that," he said.

"Not me," I said. "You'd be the one making up poems."

The pleasure of that thought settled at the corners of his mouth, and I rested my head lightly against his shoulder. I was sure I could hear his heart beating.

Then an odd uneasiness, like the swollen silence just before a thunderclap, crept over me.

"What's wrong?" Samson pulled away to look at me.

"I . . . nothing."

I knew the feeling though—something bad was headed my way.

I'd just finished sweeping up in the kitchen when I heard Naomi's car. It was dark out, past ten, and I'd forgotten to turn on the porch light. She and Aunt Birdie came around back, through the screen door into the kitchen. I expected to see Clover in tow behind them, but she wasn't there. A spasm skittered through my stomach.

Dust kicked up by the car had mingled with Naomi's perspiration and left gray streaks on her flushed, freckled face. Aunt Birdie didn't look much better. Her scrambled-egg hairdo was wilted, and damp strings of it were plastered to her forehead.

"Anybody call?" Naomi's voice rose with expectation.

I shook my head.

Aunt Birdie stepped around me, touching my arm gently. "Let me fix you a bite to eat," she said to Naomi.

Naomi looked at her as though Birdie had lost her mind. "I'm supposed to eat?" she snapped, and she slumped down onto one of the chairs. "Lordy, I can't bear the thought of my baby all alone out there . . . in the dark . . . God knows where . . . maybe hurt . . . maybe calling me."

Aunt Birdie leaned over, trying to hug her, but Naomi straightened up. Birdie stepped back, her face anxious and pained.

Naomi's fingers began tracing over the yellow-and-green daisy pattern on the vinyl tablecloth. Then she stopped dead still, staring ahead of her as though something had just registered in her brain. Slowly she turned to the chair by the sink counter, and she looked at Rosie's broken-necked, caved-in guitar resting on the seat. Its twisted, arching strings quivered slightly each time the fan oscillated by. She turned her head back and lifted her eyes to mine.

"What went on here this morning, Memphis?"

When I'd gathered up the crippled guitar and brought it down to the kitchen earlier, I was sure I was braced for whatever Naomi would dish out. But the hard edge of her voice set off an alarm in my head. I stood silent.

She twisted around and grabbed me by the wrist. "What went on, Memphis?"

In an instant Aunt Birdie had her arms around me and jerked me away. "Stop it, Naomi!" She looked at me. "Get on up to your room, honey. It's been a long day, and everybody's frazzled. Let me talk to your grandmama about this."

Naomi's eyes blazed. "You're going to explain this girl to *me?*"

I stumbled out of the kitchen and fled up the darkened stairs.

The bed beckoned like an ocean of sorrow, and I threw myself down and pushed my face into the musty, faded chenille coverlet and tried to cry. Nothing would come, just a hard burning in my chest. Why was it *always* my fault?

If I knew where John Riley was, I thought, I'd take my egg money, walk up to the highway, and flag down the next Greyhound bus before Naomi could even figure out I was gone. Just get out. Never look back. She sure wouldn't be sending out any search parties for me—we'd just all heave a sigh of relief.

I asked Naomi once if John Riley ever wrote. She pursed her lips tight and went on reading the newspaper as if she didn't hear me. Aunt Birdie told me later that yes, he did write every once in a while. Sometimes from Texas, sometimes from Nevada, and once from California. No, never from New Orleans. And yes, he did send money— not a lot, but some. But as far as she knew, it had been quite awhile since Naomi had heard from him.

Sometimes at night, as I lay drifting on the rim of sleep, New Orleans came whispering through the dark. I could see myself, barefoot and raggy-butt, comfortable in my baby skin and happy as a sidewalk weed. I could catch the stomach-rumbling smells of fried okra balls and simmering gumbo drifting up through our open apartment windows from Archie's Café downstairs. And in my deepest mind, I saw flickering flashes of Rosie, John Riley, and me sitting on a bench in the little corner park, eating boiled peanuts, sucking every last trace of salt out of the moist, earthy hulls. Our heads and feet were keeping time with Easy Tucker's lowdown blues guitar, and John Riley, as if he was worshipping some kind of god, dropped our last fifty cents into Easy's sweat-stained fedora.

Those ragged memories, prowling like bony cats through the back alleys of my mind, were getting harder to hang on to. I tried to conjure up a picture of John Riley, but it kept shifting. More and more it was like finding an old photo at the bottom of a drawer and wondering, for just a second, *Who is this?*

What was John Riley doing right now, this very minute? Was he thinking of me?

I rolled over and stared out the window at a hail of stars swirling across the deep purple sky.

The phone downstairs woke me during the night. Footsteps rushed to answer. I raised up, bracing my weight on my elbows, and strained to hear the urgent tangle of voices. There seemed to be three or four people down there. One was a man, but I couldn't figure out who he was. Then it grew quiet again. The pungent aroma of fresh coffee seeped through the darkness, and the only sound was the soft clicking of cups on the kitchen table.

What was Clover trying to prove? Why didn't she just come on out from wherever she was hiding and get it over with? Naomi was never going to blame her for anything. Didn't she know that by now? She was standing right there last year when Naomi threatened to ship me upstate to some home for wayward girls if I didn't stop agitating Clover. Aunt Birdie said it was just an idle threat, that Naomi was mad at the world because her life was in a shambles. But I worried just the same.

Off in the distance, thunder rumbled forward, carrying with it a cool breeze that lured me to the window. A brilliant vein of lightning lit up the pines on the hill and cracked with such ferocity I thought the sky had shattered.

There was a cry downstairs, then the screen door slammed. Naomi was in the front yard, running back and forth screaming, "No! No!" A sharp knot rose in my throat, and I remembered the terrible howling the Johnsons' dog had made when they gave away her last puppy.

"Please," I whispered, "don't let it rain."

4

I knew I was dreaming, caught in a dark, shifting world of empty gray streets and lurking terrors. Clover's voice called in an endless, plaintive wail that spiraled up out of the deep. I bolted upright in bed, squinting against the sun's morning glare, and took in the familiar pieces of my room.

Over on the dresser top sat my trolls, grown darker with age, their stiff white hair incapable of wilting even in the middle of July. They stared back at me reproachfully. *We have nothing to do with this,* they seemed to be saying. I heard someone walk through the downstairs hallway into the kitchen, then water running. Was Clover back?

I'll go downstairs, I thought, and there she'll be, sitting at the table, eating Rice Krispies out of her old blue flowered bowl, her bedraggled coonskin cap lying next to her like a dead squirrel. I'll control myself and say, "Hey, Clover," and she'll pretend she doesn't hear me as usual. We'll muddle through as if yesterday had never happened. Naomi, coming in with the egg basket, will see how calm and reasonable I am, and maybe she'll give me a little thank-you nod the way that grownups do with each other. And that will be a start, anyway. Aunt Birdie's always saying it's never too late to start over.

But Clover wasn't in the kitchen—Mrs. Preacher Dalton was. She'd cocked the fan just enough to keep its oscillating breeze from fuzzing up her nest of pale brown curls. She was more pregnant than ever—this had to be the fourth time. Something always went wrong, though, and she never brought any babies home from the hospital. I could almost feel sorry for her, if she wasn't forever trying to pick through my brain as if I was some outlandish specimen never before seen in these parts.

"Oh," I said. "I thought I heard Clover."

She was poised, waiting for me. "Well, let's hope that's not the wishful thinking of a guilty conscience."

She was sitting at the kitchen table, grading Sunday school lessons. Her large gray eyes, naked as boiled eggs, took in my buzzy hair and bare feet, and a tic of disapproval twitched at one corner of her mouth. She flipped through the lesson sheets and pulled one out, studying it with pursed lips.

"No," she said finally. "Poor little Clover is apparently lost—or worse."

"Why are you calling her 'poor little Clover'?" A string of perspiration slid down the back of my neck and inched along my spine. I reached around with one hand and squashed it against my flimsy nightgown.

"Because she's one of life's sad, sad little ones. A lamb with her own cross to bear. And now she's apparently lost—or worse."

I couldn't help snorting under my breath. Anybody who'd spent much time around Clover would never in a million years call her a sad little lamb.

"She's hiding," I said. "She does it all the time."

Mrs. Preacher Dalton looked up at me and sieved air through the gap between her front teeth. "You mean she's stayed away all night before?"

"Well, no, not all night. But long enough."

"Why do you think she does that?" She tilted her head to one side, her eyes suddenly bright and sharp as a jay hawk's.

"How should I know? To make me look like a jackass, I reckon."

"I hope you're not being sassy with me. I'm just trying to . . ." She fell silent, watching the tips of her fingers gently stroke her swollen belly.

"Where's Naomi?" I blurted out.

She flinched. "Is that a nice way to speak of your grandmother?"

"That's the way she wants it."

Rosie, John Riley, and I had always called each other by our given names, and when I came here, I'd just started calling Naomi by hers. She'd never said not to. But was that Mrs. Preacher Dalton's business?

The phone rang.

"Maybe I better get that," she said. She struggled to her feet. But I reached around to the wall and picked up the receiver. She stood there, her eyebrows raised, waiting for me to hand it over.

"Hello?" I said, turning away from her.

"Hey, Memphis," said Samson. "Clover come out of hiding yet?"

"Nope."

"What's wrong? Oh . . . somebody there?"

"Yep."

"Call me when you get a chance?"

"O.K."

Mrs. Preacher Dalton had eased back down on the chair, her stomach bulging out in front of her. It was weird thinking a person was growing in there, and for a minute I felt sorry for it. If it beat the odds and made it into this world alive, it would forever be under the scrutiny of her big, bland eyes.

"That was your friend, the Greeley boy?"

"Maybe."

She sieved air in through her front teeth again. "I'm surprised your grandmama's still letting you run so free with him. You're both getting too big, and folks are already starting to talk."

I knew what she meant, and the thought of it made my face burn.

"His name's Samson, not 'Greeley boy,'" I said, offended by the way she referred to him as though he wasn't quite on the up and up.

It was Samson who'd stood by me through my first year at school in Blue Parrot. I could read and write and knew my arithmetic tables, but I'd never been to a real school before. That first day, with knees of jelly and my stomach doing flip-flops, I scooted to the back of the bus and tried not to look scared. When Samson got on, he came right down the aisle and sat next to me.

"You're the New Orleans girl," he said, announcing it instead of asking. I liked that. It made me feel special.

Rebecca Simmons, Queen of the In-Crowd, wouldn't rest until she'd put me in my place. Her daddy owned the Dixie Mart, and she and her friends always sat in a huddle at one of the picnic tables in the schoolyard, tittering behind their hands and throwing smirky glances at the Outies, the group to which I'd quickly been relegated. One day, after a week of trying to stare me down, she said real loud, "I didn't even know they let hippies in Blue Parrot."

Her friends all broke up laughing.

A couple of days later, she walked up to me with two of her friends hovering at her elbows and said, "My mama told me to stay a country mile away from the likes of you!" Her friends laughed when she dragged out the word *country*, trying to make it sound hillbilly.

"Then why don't you do that?" I said and stuck out my chin.

Shock zigzagged across her pink, bunny-rabbit face. Then her eyes turned spiteful. "You know, your grandmama tells folks your mama died from a brain bubble, but that don't change the truth. My mama said it was more like a *drug* bubble." She leaned in toward me, the scent of her genteel cologne rising like mist from her curly blond hair. "I guess dirty hippie druggies get just what they deserve!"

Without even thinking, I popped her in the mouth, splitting her lip and sending flecks of blood down the front of her dress. Samson tried to take the blame for it, but Miss Ferguson wasn't buying. I was suspended for a week.

Aunt Birdie and Naomi were on the front porch sorting through a big flat of lima beans when Miss Ferguson showed up the next day to discuss my disruptive behavior and what would be expected from me when I returned. Samson and I were up in the oak tree, eating sugar-and-butter sandwiches, listening to every word.

Naomi didn't say much as Miss Ferguson perched on the edge of a straight-backed chair and droned on and on. Aunt Birdie got restless, though, shifting around in her chair, frowning every so often and working her mouth like she was hoping to get a word in. Finally she interrupted.

"We're talking about a child who has recently lost her parents," she said. "Could we cut a slice of kindness here?"

When I went back to school, I had to stand up in front of everyone and apologize, and Miss Ferguson said, "Thank you, Memphis. We trust this kind of behavior will not be happening again."

Rebecca Simmons and her friends left me alone after that, even though they sometimes muttered "trash" when I walked by.

Samson told me to pay them no mind, but after I hit Rebecca Simmons in the mouth, it was as if I had a big sign on my back: *Watch out! Here comes trouble.* It didn't seem to make any difference what I said or did; my reputation as a hardhead was signed and sealed, Blue Parrot gospel. When Mrs. Preacher Dalton got wind of my sorry state, she took it upon herself to try and rectify my moral compass whenever she got the chance. I was forever dipping and dodging to avoid her, but I was miserably trapped—to her evangelical delight—every Sunday morning at ten o'clock.

The percolator started bubbling and rumbling, and the sharp aroma of brewing coffee billowed into the room.

"Mmm, that smells so good." Mrs. Preacher Dalton gave me a pretend smile, but I didn't smile back. "You're a strange girl, Memphis Riley. I'd have to say downright puzzling sometimes." She studied my face as though looking for any small sign of redemption, anything at all worth saving.

"You know, if you want to talk about what happened here yesterday between you and poor little Clover . . ."

"I'll just ask Aunt Birdie," I said.

"What?" Her face went blank.

"I'll ask Aunt Birdie where Naomi is." I headed for the screen door.

"You're going outside like that?"

I paused, looking back at her over my shoulder. A flicker of spitefulness nudged me. "Uh-huh," I said and smiled at her for the first time.

Did she think I was so stupid all she had to do was flutter her make-believe wings and I'd fall to my knees blabbing my heart out, begging forgiveness for whatever my sins were supposed to be? Couldn't the Lord see for Himself what was going on and either smile on me or strike me down?

"Well, Miss Birdie isn't home either," Mrs. Preacher Dalton said. "They're all down at the church, deciding who looks where." She paused, then smiled slightly when I turned back to her. "Poor little Clover's been gone too long now. They're having to get serious. A couple of the Knockleys said they saw her out by Moody Bog late yesterday.

"Course we all know what a bunch of liars they are." She groaned mournfully. "The Lord *hates* liars. He really does. But you never know; it could be true. Very disturbing. Anyway, your grandmama says you're not to leave the house."

"And *you're* my guard?"

"Oh, Memphis, see, that's what I mean. Don't you think that remark was uncalled for? I just volunteered to keep you company in case . . ."

"In case of what?"

She flushed and rolled her eyes toward the ceiling. Then she shook her head as if, no, there really wasn't much hope for the likes of me.

I stared at her, wondering why she always seemed to go out of her way to make me feel bad about myself. At Sunday school she'd say things like, "The diligent gardener digs those weeds out before they spoil the garden— something you should consider, Memphis." This would generally be accompanied by snickers around the room.

"What are you staring at me like that for?" Her mouth twitched.

"I was wondering . . . does the Lord really see inside people's hearts?"

"What a wonderful thing to put one's mind to! Why don't we talk about that?" Her voice was sugary with expectation.

She got up, moved the noisy percolator to a cold burner, and turned off the gas. Her perfectly ironed cotton dress was already wilting; rings of perspiration showed at the armpits, and its back stuck to her rump. She pulled it loose, shook it out lightly, then took a cup from the drainboard.

At the table she stirred two heaping spoons of sugar into her coffee and lifted the steaming cup to her mouth. Her eyes were lit with triumph. Victory at last—she was about to reel me in.

I poured myself the last of the day-old lemonade and set the empty pitcher in the sink. I knew she thought I was going to sit at the table with her, and I heard her give a grunt of surprise when the screen door slapped shut behind me.

I needed to sort things out. I sat on the back steps and washed down the lemonade, trying to push away the spidery thoughts that crept out of the dark corners of my mind. *Moody Bog? Why would Clover be there? Could something . . . ?*

There seemed to be an oddness in the air, as though something had shifted—even the trees looked slanty. I pulled my knees up close and laid my head against my arms. *Let her come walking across the yard now, Lord. Let this all be over now.*

But the only sound was the faint, drawn-out clucking of a hen stirring on her nest.

Slowly it dawned on me that I hadn't seen the guitar in the kitchen when I came down. What had Naomi done with it? I got up and went back inside.

Mrs. Preacher Dalton was still at the kitchen table, looking at her watch and listening for the sound of anybody's car in the driveway. She seemed all played out, her patient, practiced expression frayed around the edges. She'd put away her papers, and her fake-leather satchel leaned against a chair leg.

"Have you seen my guitar?" I asked. "It was broken, lying on that chair."

A slight frown creased her forehead. "Shouldn't you be getting some clothes on?" She didn't look too good. Her face was beaded with perspiration, and the lavender shadows beneath her eyes seemed darker.

"No, I haven't seen any guitar." She touched her stomach. "Look, Memphis, I have to go. My little precious is getting restless, and I need to get off my feet."

I felt a twinge of guilt for being so contrary and I sure didn't want to be the cause of another little Dalton changing its mind.

"You can lie down on the sofa in the living room," I said. "I'll turn on the floor fan."

"Oh, that is just so kind of you, Memphis, but it'd probably be best if I . . ." Her words ragged off.

"Can I help you to your car?"

"That'd be nice. It's probably just the coffee, don't you know. Probably just an upset stomach, but I can't take any chances with this one." Her eyes glistened. "You don't mind, do you? You'll be a good girl and stay put like your grandmama said?"

"Yes, ma'am." I grabbed up her satchel and eased her along to the door. "Sure you don't need me to go with you?" I could have bitten off my tongue, but from the look on her face, I could tell all she wanted was to get away from me, the sooner the better.

I waved good-bye from the driveway and watched her pull onto the road and head into town. As I walked back around to the kitchen, a blue jay in the oak tree let out a harsh scream, then swooped toward me like the hand of God. I ducked, flailing my arms, and ran for the screen door.

5

A nervous bubble settled in the pit of my stomach as I eased open the door to Clover's room. Not even Naomi went in and out of there as she pleased. It was Clover's private territory. Every Friday morning she took a bucket of hot water, brushes, and a mop to it, scrubbing every inch over and over, sometimes spending three or four hours in there with the door closed. She was the same way with her laundry, washing it over and over until Naomi would finally say in a praising way, "That really looks clean, Clover."

The room was where she kept her boxes. They were mostly smaller sizes in different shapes and colors. She'd been saving them for years and had them stacked in three columns on the floor beside her dresser. Some were tied with string, a few with ribbon, and some had thick rubber bands around them. Aunt Birdie said once that Clover was a pack rat. When I asked what that was, she said it was a very pretty rat with big, bright eyes and soft fur; it loved to collect pieces of paper, sticks, seeds, anything shiny and haul the stuff off to its nest. She said when a ring or brooch turned up missing, more than likely it was sitting behind the walls with the pack rat.

I'd just gotten up the nerve to step into the room and had my hand on the doorknob when I thought I heard footsteps on the back porch. I quickly backed out into the hallway. The last thing I wanted was for Clover to catch me snooping through her stuff.

I decided to go downstairs and try to act glad to see her, though I was never going to forgive her for the guitar—never. But the edginess that had been setting in for the last twenty-four hours was getting scary, and I realized I *would* be glad to see her, if only to get things back to square one.

The confusing thing was, when I found she wasn't downstairs, I was relieved that I didn't have to deal with her. I decided to go on over to Samson's but stopped at the kitchen sink for a drink of water first. When I lifted the glass to my mouth, I felt a difference in the air around me—a strange odor. I turned and saw a runty man watching me through the screen door.

"'Cuse me, miss. Hope I didn't scare you." His squinty eyes flicked around the kitchen. "It's almighty blazin' out here t'day. Could you spare me a glass of that, too?"

His dirt-etched, weathered skin and filthy, ragged clothes seemed to blend into each other so that you could barely tell where one left off and the other started. A twisted, sweat-stained bandanna was tied around his creased forehead and held down his stringy gray hair, except for some wispy strands on top that looked like the brackish air fern at the edge of Moody Bog.

When I walked toward him with the glass of water, his stench—sour, salty, and faintly pissy—turned my stomach.

I opened the screen just enough to hand him the glass and watched the big Adam's apple in his skinny throat bob up and down as he drained it without taking it from his lips.

"Would 'nother be too much to ask?" His breath stunk as though something had died inside his mouth.

I hesitated, and he gave me a sly, hangdog smile. His teeth were snaggled, brown with tobacco and rot, and I noticed the stains and healed-over blisters on his smoking fingers. He was a hard-time man, sucking each cigarette down to his knuckles.

"Don't reckon you got anything left over from supper last night?"

"I'll get you a plate." It was our way with hard-time folks. "Don't like to see anybody go hungry." I felt kind of high-flown and thought, If only folks like Mrs. Preacher Dalton could see me now, with my good spirit and kind heart.

"Well, I haven't ate in a day or two, if you call that hungry." When his coy smile relaxed, white lines splayed out from the bottom of the deep wrinkles around his eyes, giving him a strange, animal expression.

"I can tell you're a kind soul," he said.

I thought he sounded fakey, and when I looked at him, his eyes widened in mock surprise as though he'd read my mind. I felt a light catch in my throat.

"Why don't you go sit on the steps," I said. "I'll bring it out."

I piled up a plate with chicken wings and potato salad and took it out to him with another glass of water. I stepped back inside and flipped the latch on the screen door.

"My oh my, now this is a feast, a bona fidey treat for this hungry old stomach." He lit into the food like a half-starved road dog. When he was done, he ran a dirty finger around his gums, getting every particle of food loose, rolling it around on his tongue as though he was identifying it before he swallowed it. Then he let out a big belch.

"I do thank you, Miss." He pushed out a long, loud sigh and began thrumming his fingers against his full belly.

"Just came in off the road yonder." He lifted his chin toward the highway. "Been campin' out, you know, summer and all, but y'all got kudzu 'long there. A man got to be careful that dang stuff don't reach out and grab him by the throat while he's sleepin'." He turned and looked at me.

It was an old joke in these parts—don't sleep with your windows open if there's kudzu close by. The stubborn, rubbery vines wound around everything in sight and sometimes grew as much as a foot a day. Aunt Birdie said it was a good thing the frost killed it every winter, or else we'd all be running for our lives. But every spring it came back from root like a bad promise.

"Well, I best get goin'." He pulled himself up, but instead of heading down the steps, he sidled like a crab over to the door, pressed his forehead against the screen, and stared at me.

I stepped back, and my hand moved up to check the latch.

"You home by yourself?"

"No. No, I'm not."

"Oh? Where's the missus?"

"Upstairs . . ."

"And she's been hearin' all the goin's-on and ain't come down to check?"

"Daddy . . ." I said and heard my voice tremble. "She's giving Daddy a haircut."

"Oh, Daddy's home, too, huh? Bet he's a big old booger and just got through cleanin' his shotgun."

"You better get on along now." I tried to sound firm like Naomi, but it came out thin and wishy-washy.

"Oooeee, see how you done turned on Old Roy. That's a doggone shame." His eyelids drooped, and he pushed his forehead harder against the screen. "You gettin' scared, ain't you, Miss Do-Goody? Next thing you know, you gonna be wee-weeing your pants."

Fear was rising in me like a flood tide. Something bad was happening.

He grabbed the screen-door handle and rattled it. "This piece of flimsy crap can't keep me out, li'l darlin'." He shook the door again, so hard I thought he was jerking it open. "You ain't a good liar, neither," he taunted. "Ain't no cars in the driveway. Ain't a sound round here but you and me."

But there *was* another sound: three loud rings of Samson's bicycle bell. Our signal. It meant he was heading up the driveway. I whirled and raced through the house and stumbled out the front door.

Samson took one look at me and skidded to a stop.

"What's wrong?" He threw his bike to the ground and ran toward me.

"There's an old creep on the back porch, and he was, you know . . ."

Samson's chunky body seemed to grow a foot, and his thick black eyebrows knotted together.

"He hurt you?" He took off round the side of the house.

"Wait," I cried. "He's creepy, Samson. Watch out!" I dashed off after him.

The old man was gone. Samson stood flatfooted and red-faced, looking round the empty yard. I walked over to the porch. The plate I'd piled for the man was on the top step where he'd left it, the chicken bones gnawed clean and chewed up into little pieces. His stench hung in the air.

Samson walked over and wrinkled his nose. "You sure that wasn't some kind of swamp thing?"

"Oh, Lord," I said, looking down at the thin thread of urine trickling along the inside of my leg. "I've peed my pants."

We both looked toward the back door—we'd seen our share of late-night horror movies on TV with *things* lurking in closets. No way was either of us going inside the house.

"Hurry and grab those jeans off that nail," I said, pointing down the porch. "We can get up in the tree and see Deputy Bowen if he swings down off the highway."

I made him turn around while I changed and thought, If only Mrs. Preacher Dalton could see us now, she'd probably faint dead away.

"Hurry!" he cried.

"I'm hurrying! I'm hurrying!"

We weren't halfway up the tree before I spotted the man shagging along the highway.

"You sure that's him?" Samson asked.

"Yeah, he's got that red thing tied around his head." We watched him until he was out of sight.

Naomi and Aunt Birdie pulled in about half an hour later. They both looked beat.

"We'll keep going," Aunt Birdie was saying. "She couldn't have gotten too far." She hurried to keep up with Naomi. "Everybody has their eyes open, and I bet we hear back before too long. She might've just got turned around, you know?" She glanced over at Samson's bicycle sprawled in the front yard. "I got a feeling we'll be getting some feedback pretty soon. Sheriff Wilson's got all his deputies on the lookout. And all those folks we talked to this morning—must have been six or eight cars at the Chicken Shack alone. Word's spreading, Naomi, you'll see. Clover'll be back before you know it."

Naomi didn't answer. She walked ahead of Aunt Birdie with her head ducked down and her arms wrapped tight around her waist as if she was holding in a stomachache. She didn't even hold the door open for Aunt Birdie, who ran up on the porch and grabbed it before it slammed shut.

"Don't that just take it?" I said. "Naomi's acting like it's the end of the world. You know as well as I do that Clover's just holed up somewhere around here, probably scared to come out now she's been gone so long."

"I don't know." Samson cut his eyes away from mine. "I think she'd be getting awful hungry and tired by now."

"You just don't get it, Samson. She's good at this! She could probably outlast all of us." My voice was rough with irritation, but somewhere inside my head, his words rang true.

"Memphis!" Aunt Birdie called from the front porch. "You out there?"

"You gonna tell them about that old creep?" Samson dropped down to a lower branch, then grabbed hold of a thick rope knotted around the bottom limb and slid to the ground.

"There y'all are," Aunt Birdie called. "Come on in, Memphis."

"If I was you, I'd tell," Samson said, and he hopped on his bike. "He might've done something to Clover."

6

Aunt Birdie put a finger to her lips, shushing me. "She's out like a light," she whispered, "worn to a frazzle."

Naomi was lying on the sofa with her shoes off and a damp towel across her forehead, covering her eyes. The big floor fan in the far corner rattled and whirred like an airplane propeller, churning the air across the ceiling and sending nervous ripples and flutters down the ivory lace curtains. In the doorway across the room, Aunt Birdie crooked a finger and motioned for me to follow her. I glanced down at Naomi as I passed. She seemed smaller than usual and thinner, and her breathing came in fits and starts.

Aunt Birdie's shoulders drooped, and her face was drawn, older-looking. "We need to talk, honey," she said, nudging me ahead of her into the kitchen. "This thing is eating her up."

I never could figure out how Birdie and Naomi came to be such good friends. Aunt Birdie said Naomi was a different person when she was young—that life had dealt her a hard hand. I tried to connect with that, but she'd made it plain I was a pain in her life and she'd just as soon I hadn't shown up.

Aunt Birdie never had a husband or children, and she lived in the same house she'd been born and grown up in. She said when her parents got old and close to their going time, things had changed, and she'd become the mama. They died within two days of each other when they were way up in their eighties. She said it was a blessing that one didn't leave the other behind to grieve and be alone. I asked her how come she didn't get married after that. She said the one she wanted had gotten away.

I poured her a glass of iced tea and made her a ham-and-pickle sandwich. She was hungry and chewed too fast. When she saw me watching, she set the sandwich down.

"Whoa," she said, "let me slow down here before this all comes upchucking. I'm just too tired to put one foot in front of the other." She glanced at the plastic black-and-white cat clock above the sink. Every time its tail ticked, its big eyes tocked. "Click on the radio, hon', let's see if they put Clover on the news."

Jim Simpson's County Roundup was just starting.

The Jackson County Sheriff's office reported today that Blue Parrot resident Clover Martin has been missing from her home since yesterday morning. The twenty-nine-year-old mentally handicapped woman was last seen on Blue Parrot Road at approximately eleven A.M., walking in the direction of Johnson's General Store. At the time of her disappearance, Martin, who is just over five feet tall and weighs approximately ninety pounds, was wearing a red-and-white-striped T-shirt and blue denim skirt. She was either wearing or carrying her childhood keepsake, a 1950s Davy Crockett coonskin cap. Anyone with information is asked to call the sheriff's office in Oaklee.

On a lighter note, Teri Lee Butler of Prineville captured the Miss . . .

I had a hard time getting this through my head. All these people thought Clover was really missing—even the radio station in Oaklee. I looked at Aunt Birdie as she finished her sandwich, picking up the crumbs with the tip of her finger and pressing them to her tongue.

"But she's just hiding," I croaked.

"No, Memphis," she said softly. "I don't think so."

I stared down at my hands, picking at a tiny scab on one of my knuckles. *Really missing?*

Aunt Birdie leaned over and patted my arm. "Sheriff Wilson's going to stop by in a little while to talk to you. You understand?"

"What about?"

"He just wants to get a handle on things."

What did that mean?

"You want to talk with me about the guitar? About the argument?" She patted my arm again to get my attention. "Memphis?"

"There was an old man here today." I didn't look up.

"What do you mean, an old man?"

"A hard-time man. Off the highway. Called himself Old Roy."

Her breathing picked up, and she leaned in closer. "Here?"

"Yeah. I gave him something to eat, then he . . . turned mean."

"Merciful Lord! What happened?"

"Samson came by and scared him off. He was really creepy."

"Who was creepy?" Naomi stood in the doorway, barefoot, her short, graying hair stuck in damp curls around her face.

In a flash, Aunt Birdie answered, "Not who. What! Memphis was just telling me about a spider's nest round the side of the house."

Naomi grunted softly and flopped to a chair. "This thing is a nightmare," she said, and she propped her chin on the heel of her hand. "I feel like my whole insides are caving away." She looked over at me, studying my face, then frowned and turned away.

"Let me fix you a cup of Lady Althea's tea." That was Aunt Birdie's way of getting Naomi's attention away from me. Lady Althea was a root woman living in a run-down trailer way up on the other side of town. She was kin to the Tremaynes, the black folks who ran a cane farm up there. Her tea was Blue Parrot's cupboard remedy for headaches and nerves.

As Aunt Birdie bustled about making the tea, she kept up a gentle, running chatter. "You have to eat something, Naomi. Can't let yourself run down too far. It's hard, it sure is, but you're strong. We'll all get through this. There

Pedro M~~~~~~~
H. S. !

we go." She set the cup down in front of Naomi. "It's not too hot; drink it all. You really do need to go on back and stretch out."

Naomi sipped the tea, and they talked over where they'd been that morning, all the way past Oaklee to the south and then backtracking and going about sixty miles north to Abbotsville, stopping at every service station, diner, hamburger joint, road stand, rest stop, you name it. They picked apart what people had said, how they'd looked at Clover's picture, how some of them squinted and studied, giving Naomi hope, then shook their heads—no, sorry, sure will keep an eye out.

"They put a report on the county news," said Aunt Birdie. "We heard it."

Naomi nodded halfheartedly. "The thing that gets me," she said, "is how some folks around here are acting like Clover's just off somewhere playing."

My ears stung, but I sat still, eyes lowered. *How could Naomi not know after all this time how Clover really was?*

"I know her," she said. "I mean, who knows her better than I? I raised her, didn't I?" She had her finger hooked around the cup handle, sliding the teacup back and forth in front of her on the tablecloth.

The phone rang, and Aunt Birdie jumped up.

"I see," she said into the receiver. "Yes, I'll tell her." She stood holding the receiver for a minute as though trying to find just the right words.

"That was Georgene Johnson. She said some of the men have decided to go out and check around Moody Bog just in case the Knockleys were telling the truth."

"Merciful God," whispered Naomi, closing her eyes.

Aunt Birdie went over to her and stroked the damp curls off her forehead. "It's a good idea, honey. It's gonna be all right, you'll see. Just one less place to worry about."

"Is it that fool Deputy Bowen who's coming by or the sheriff?" Naomi looked up at the clock.

Aunt Birdie cut her eyes over at me, and I saw a flicker of worry, maybe even fear, cross her face. "It's probably gonna be Sheriff Wilson. Why don't you go stretch out again?"

"I don't want to fall asleep," Naomi said. "I want to be wide awake when he gets here." She glanced at me, then looked away quickly.

I watched a vein at the side of her forehead swell and throb and I had the oddest feeling it was all she could do to control herself, that maybe when they were out there in the old Falcon, driving up and down the highway, Aunt Birdie had told her to lay off me. I had to get out of there. I felt as though a big invisible hand was pushing me into a corner.

Naomi started forward in her chair when I stood up. "Where are you going?"

"Put my library books out in the pickup box," I lied. "The truck'll be by this afternoon."

Naomi's eyes widened. "You're worrying about *library books* at a time like this?"

I ducked my head and edged toward the door.

Outside, I grabbed my bike from the side of the porch, hopped on, and sailed down the driveway onto Blue Parrot Road. I couldn't believe they were actually going to search way out at Moody Bog. I banked in at Aunt Birdie's house, along the other side of her pecan grove, and gave three loud rings on my bicycle bell. It wouldn't take Samson long to catch up with me. I headed out across the back field to Moody Bog. I had to see this for myself.

Almost everywhere you went back of Blue Parrot's pine woods, sooner or later you were going to be jumping one of the McColl River's straggly little creeks. They all fed into the swamp about two miles west of town. It was called Moody Bog and was off limits to kids. There were red-bellied snakes, grownups said, maybe even alligators—and restless spirits of long-ago slaves who'd been trapped there after making a run for it. Their ghostly lights glowed throughout the swamp at night, they said. We shivered at these things, but they might as well have told some of us not to breathe as to stay away from Moody Bog. The swamp was a Pied Piper.

At first I was afraid of it, but after a while it came to be like some ancient church grown from the earth before there were people. Its canopy of pines and live oaks met way up overhead, dripping down Spanish moss laced with wild pink and white azaleas. Every living thing in there knew when you showed up. The birds flew out like sentinels from the marsh grass in a noisy rush of wings, chattering and screeching as they disappeared into the shadows.

If you stood still for a while, rabbits and possums and bandit-faced raccoons came out of hiding, slipping in and around great fanning ferns and six-foot-tall stalks of blood-red flowers. Frogs and toads plopped in and out of the tea-brown water, and pretty little lizards posed on wet slicks and darted off at the first startle. Even on the hottest day, it was cool and shadowy inside. But it wasn't a place to let your guard down. You had to keep your eyes open and stay up on the boardwalks. The murky water beneath the lily pads was alive with eels and snakes on the prowl. You could always tell by a stomach-turning, rotten smell where something dead was tangled in the weeds that undulated up from the bottom.

It didn't take long for Samson to catch up with me. As we coaxed our bikes across one knotty field after another, I couldn't seem to connect with what was going on. Things were happening too fast, and none of it seemed real. The stagnant odor of Moody Bog seeped through the stand of pines just ahead and tainted the humid air. Scattered at the edge of the field, old pieces of rusted-out farm machinery were strewn about like the bones of prehistoric swamp creatures. Everything seemed larger than usual, out of focus, changing even as I looked at it.

Finally my legs gave out, and I threw my bike down and flopped on the ground, flushed and exhausted.

Up ahead, Samson looked over his shoulder, walked his bike back, and trampled down the thatchy yellow grass around me. "Might be snakes," he said and blotted his sweaty face against the shoulder of his T-shirt.

Coming toward us from beyond the pines was the muffled sound of people calling back and forth to one another and the occasional roar of a pickup engine. Every so often we heard the crack of a rifle and a man's voice shouting, "Got it!"

"I can't believe they're really in there looking for her," I said.

"Yeah." Samson squatted down across from me.

We sat thinking that over for a while.

"Everything seems so messed up," I said. "I mean, that old creep showing up on the back porch and all . . ."

He nodded and looked away.

"Something else," I said and waited for him to look back. "The sheriff wants to talk to me."

He studied me for a minute. "Aw, they do that all the time—like on *Hawaii Five-O*."

"Yeah, but it's with people like Wo Fat, ones they suspect of something. Why would he want to talk to me?"

"I don't know. 'Cause you saw her leave?"

Without any warning, I burst out crying.

Samson's mouth dropped open in surprise. He'd seen me stand a lot of ground and not shed one tear. I guess you're either a crier or you're not. Sometimes I've tried to cry to let off steam—kind of like old man Jenson trying to knock loose a sticky valve on the school boiler. But I always came up dry as a bone. Now here I was, flooded, and I didn't know if it was for Clover or for my own helpless sense of being caught in something going deadly wrong.

My flash-flood tears dried up just as fast as they'd started, leaving my eyes feeling tight and stiff behind puffy eyelids.

Beyond the pines, the noisy searchers poked through the swamp, looking for something that didn't belong there. And the swamp, like a hoary old alligator, lay waiting for any one of them to make a false move. There wasn't one place inside my head that was willing to believe they'd find Clover in there.

Samson stood up and blotted his sweaty face on his T-shirt again. "Maybe we could take a look at that possum."

All the talk at Sunday school that past week had been about the two-headed possum caged up at the root woman's place. We'd all sucked in our breath when Jimmy Harrel said he'd seen it, his agitated whisper tumbling out the tale of how he'd snuck up on it, coming in the back way through the stand of pines bordering the Tremayne line.

Lady Althea Tremayne's dilapidated trailer hunkered in among those trees like an aging mountain cat, just far enough back to keep it hidden from casual eyes. She didn't like people poking around her place, not even her own folks. If riled enough, she was known to chase off more than one irritating ignoramus by swinging a big snake like a whip.

"Jimmy said the cage is almost up to the fence. We wouldn't have to go on her place." Samson stood waiting for my answer.

"I saw a two-headed baby snake once in Baton Rouge," I said. "In a tent show."

"Naw!"

"It was jarred up like pigs' feet, only it was a snake, and the brine looked like sewer water. Both its mouths were wide open." I made up the part about the mouths being open and was immediately sorry.

"I wonder if it was alive when they put it in the jar." There he was again with that look on his face. I'd decided long ago that Samson was born to be somebody big in the animal world.

"I was just kidding," I said. "I didn't see that."

"Yeah, you did."

We headed off across the field, walking our bikes through the dull, hot afternoon toward Lady Althea's place. The unsettling noises of Clover's search party faded behind us, and we ambled along in our own silence.

I knew I should've been heading back to the house, but I didn't want to talk to any sheriff. I was going to be blamed for something that was at least half Clover's fault. But with all this ruckus now, the blame would *all* be dumped on me.

Overhead, a marsh hawk made a lazy pass, then circled around and came back, dipping and gliding as though in love with its own graceful shadow.

Oh, to fly away! When I was ten, I made up a song for John Riley: *John Riley, John Riley, where do you roam? Your daughter's in trouble and needs to come home.* I hummed it to myself now. *Do you ever think of me, John Riley?*

7

We came up on one of the McColl's twisty creeks and ran toward it, tearing off our sneakers so we could plunge our burning, sweaty feet into the cool water. Tiny minnows flashed through our cupped fingers as we stooped and threw handfuls of water up into our flushed faces. But Samson didn't want to tarry long, and soon we pushed on to Tremayne's.

The possum's cage was just inside the barbed wire fence, in the shade of a wide pecan tree. It was strung together from rusted chicken wire and stood up off the ground on long legs made of stripped and bound saplings. A warped board covered the top, held down with a big rock. The floor was littered with pine needles and oak leaves, some dried-out corncobs, and little turds sprinkled around like beads off a broken necklace. As we watched, a pile of leaves with a ratlike, hairless tail sticking out lifted and moved toward a corner. Then it was still. We stood motionless, waiting for it to move again.

The air was humming with insects that wove in and out of the unseen layers of their world, flitting down to the cage and buzzing back up around our heads. We spooked at every crick and crackle, afraid of coming face to face with Lady Althea. A noisy family of mockingbirds flew in, bunched up in the branches overhead, and watched us. When they rose up suddenly and took off over the pines, we both jumped, ready to run for it.

"Let's get out of here," I said.

"Come on, possum," Samson whispered, staring at the cage. "Come—on—out."

There was a sudden hush, subtle and alive, as though something was holding its breath. Then she stepped from behind a tree, at least six feet tall, in a loose dress that just skirted her rough, gnarly boots: Lady Althea. With three powerful strides, she was at the fence and filled up my eyes like the shocking faces that leap at you in your dreams. A blue dotted scarf, tied around her small, perfect head, fanned out like an enormous flower at the side of her dark face.

We were nailed to the ground, caught in the magic of a root woman's spell that was so powerful we could only stare. The pungent aroma of her secret mixings flowed in the air around her, rising up from the jumble of twining necklaces laced around her shoulders and spilling down to her waist. They carried bits of bleached bone, feathers, pieces of bent nails, and small pouches, some made of worn leather and some of colored cloth knotted round with string and wire. She raised one hand, sinewy as a man's, to her face and began stroking her full lower lip, studying first me, then Samson.

"You sneakin' round to see the wonder—ain't that right?" Her voice rolled out rich and slow. She tilted her head back and stared down at us. I saw with a start that she was blind in one eye. It was milky blue and full of secrets. The other eye, the good eye, was fierce and cut you right to the bone.

"Well, let me tell you, if I was to let it out, both them mouths with all them scissor teeth would chew you up one side and down the other before you could even reckon what you come up here for."

Samson and I glanced at each other. He looked like something in a cartoon, his eyes all bugged out and a big blue vein pounding away at his temple. I could feel my legs going rubbery.

"You heard 'bout my whippety snake?"

We nodded our heads.

"And you still come up? H'm . . ." She stooped down and picked up a long twig, wrapped her fist around it, and in one down-sweeping motion, pulled it out clean of its leaves.

"Guess that gets you a look-see." She laughed, mostly to herself. "Don't know when I seen such big eyes on snoopin'-around chil'ren."

She held the switch up in front of her as though it was a magic wand, making curlicues in the air, then slid its tip through the chicken wire into the mound of leaves, flipping them back.

There it was, half-grown, hissing and spitting into the sudden light, its black-tipped fur all silvery and soft. One head was smaller than the other, growing out of the side of its neck, but both were perfect possum heads with bright, close-set eyes and long, pointed, pink-tipped noses. Both wide mouths were full of jagged little teeth. Then it rolled over on its back. Its tiny feet twitched, and then it lay still.

"Lord-a-mercy," she said with unexpected tenderness. She flipped some leaves back up on it until it was hidden. After a while we saw the leaves tremble as the possum moved into deeper cover.

"You gonna keep it in this cage?" Samson's voice had a strange, pleading edge to it, and I could tell she was taken with this tender-hearted boy.

"I didn't trap it, chile," she said to him. "I saved it." She pointed to a young pine tree down the fence. "It was up in the crux of that tree, addled, didn't know which way to go. But when it seen me, it knowed who to come to, who'd take care of it."

Samson nodded and looked up at her, his face so earnest and full of seeking I felt a kind of love for him I hadn't felt before.

"Why . . . I mean, how come . . ." His words kept sticking in his throat.

"How come it got made like this? It's a gift, chile," she said. "From the Almighty. Sometimes things that look real bad messed up is the truest of all." They locked eyes. "The minute I seen it, I knew it was a revelation, dropped right in my lap, so to speak." She looked over her shoulder, then off to each side, and she leaned in close. "I could have a mind to tell you what it signifies."

Samson and I were like two fledglings, beaks wide open, hungry, begging for nourishment.

"You think when you see somebody that the face talking to you is all there is? Is that what you think?" She lifted her head back and took in a deep breath, exhaling slowly before looking back down at us. "There's always another face behind the one talking to you. Sometimes it's a face the talker don't want you to see. Sometimes it's a face you ain't smart enough yet to see." She passed one of her strong hands over the wire cage, stroking it. "This little critter is wearing its outside face and its inside face right out here in plain sight—helpless against the cruelty of this old world." She shook her head, sucking in her cheeks. "Yes, a terrible burden! But I'll take care of it and treat it good and make sure nobody ever hurts it." Her voice began to rise, her words rumbling out like boulders. "Those that *can* has to take care of these bringers of truth!"

She stepped back, puffed herself up, and let out a deep, yowling holler that brought up the cords on her neck and sent goose bumps springing up all over me.

Samson and I jerked and leaped away from the fence, grabbing hold of each other.

"Did you step on that red rock?" she yelled at me.

The blood was pounding so hard in my head, I thought it was going to explode. Then the ground seemed to swirl and rush up to meet me. I lost my balance and fell back on my rump.

"You been out in the sun too long," she said. She cocked her head to one side and, with her good eye, peered over the fence down at a line of painted rocks.

"Yeah, looks like you stepped on that red one. Lordy-Lord, trouble comin' your way, girl." She snatched a bright purple root bag off one of her necklaces and tossed it over the fence.

"Keep this on you, girl. It'll help get you through the trouble."

Samson reached over and pulled me to my feet. We both stared down at the overturned red rock and the purple root bag.

"You chil'ren go on now." She frowned. "Don't be comin' back up here, you hear? Won't do you no good. I'm movin' this cage up to the house. Don't be tellin' nobody 'bout this baby. I got me all kinds of spells for bad chil'ren." She turned and walked away from us into the shadowy pines, holding herself tall and never once looking back.

"Gonna be a long walk back home," Samson said.

Even filtered through the oaks along Blue Parrot Road, the sun wrapped its heat around our tired bodies like elastic casing.

"Know what I was thinking back there? When she was talking 'bout the possum?"

I knew what he was going to say.

"Just shut up, Samson," I yelled. "Just shut the hell up!" I tried to surge ahead of him, but I was bone tired and could hardly push my bike along as it was. "Coming out here was a lousy idea!"

"Your idea," he said.

"Not the possum part! And for your information, no way did it remind me of Clover! Besides, you weren't the one stepped on the red rock, were you!" I had the last word, because Samson wasn't the sort to argue down to the wire.

"Wonder if I got a quarter for some root beer." He stopped and fished around in his pockets. "Nope."

"We can stop at Harrel's anyway and get a drink of water," I said.

Up ahead, at the cemetery gates, Deputy Bowen was loading ninety-year-old Hallie Benson into the back seat of his cruiser. She was about as big as a sparrow and just as dainty in her frayed silk dress, tatty straw hat, and—even in all this heat—spotless white gloves. She had herself all turned around again and couldn't figure out the way home. Her confusion had just started the year before, but folks in town looked out for her, and there was always somebody to offer her a ride or walk her home.

"You think he's out here looking for me, Sam?" My dry mouth suddenly got drier.

We watched him walk around the front of the cruiser and slide into the driver's seat. He'd only been a sheriff's deputy for about six months and spent a lot of time roaring up and down the highway as though he was headed out to a serious crime. He usually swung onto Blue Parrot Road about twice a day to check things out. Aunt Birdie said he was cuter than a bug's ear and once he settled down he'd be a fine deputy. But I didn't think he was cute. There was a mocking, squinty look to his face, as if he had a big joke on you and just might spring it when you least expected.

"Just smile and keep walking," Samson said.

When we got up to the cruiser, Deputy Bowen leaned on his elbow out the driver's window and revved the motor lightly. His eyes were hidden behind his silvery aviator sunglasses, but I knew he was giving us the once-over.

"Hope you kids haven't been up to no good," he said.

"No, sir," we said in unison.

"That's right," chimed in Mrs. Benson, craning her little puffball face up behind him. "These are very good children."

He stuck a finger to the bridge of his nose, pushed his sunglasses up onto his forehead, and peered at me. "Aren't you the Riley girl?"

"Yes, sir." I pressed my hand against Lady Althea's whiffy root bag in my jeans pocket and hoped it was working.

"What you doing clear out here on the other end of town?"

"Helping search for my aunt," I said.

"Yeah," said Samson. He shrugged his shoulders. "But we didn't come across anything."

"Yeah, well, you young-uns better get on home." Deputy Bowen lowered his sunglasses with a quick wrinkle of his forehead, then dipped his head down so he could see in his side-view mirror and smoothed back his shiny brown hair.

Tired as we were, we picked up our gait.

Deputy Bowen herded us down the gravel road all the way into town, his cruiser crunching along behind us like a big, teasing bully. At the corner of Fourth and Main, he tapped his horn and turned off to the right to take Mrs. Benson home.

"Don't be dawdling around," he called out. "Get on home now!"

The thought of a cold drink of water speeded us up toward Harrel's Drug Store on the next corner.

"Uh-oh, look," Samson murmured.

Rebecca Simmons and two of her buddies were standing in the doorway.

"Hey, Memphis, where'd you bury the body?" she hollered, and the three of them shrieked with laughter.

The shock of it stopped me in my tracks.

"Keep on walking," said Samson, grabbing hold of my wrist.

I heard Mrs. Harrel say, "That wasn't nice, Rebecca."

Samson and I trudged on by, but my heart felt like a kink of barbed wire inside my chest.

8

I recognized all the cars in the driveway—the Daltons, the Minnevers, the Easleys, the Averys—church folks who always showed up in bad times with prayers and casseroles. They were known for the power of their prayer circle—going down on their knees, holding hands, and sending up their fervent acceptance of God's will though still asking for things down here in *this* particular situation to turn out O.K. They were in there nudging God along to bring Clover home safe and sound—or else giving thanks because He had.

As I walked across the yard, my knees sagged, and I let my bicycle slide down to the ground. The house seemed strangely self-contained, as though it had closed itself against me. Then I heard the soft, lumbering hum of the air conditioner. The repair man from Oaklee had finally come around.

The kitchen door opened, and Aunt Birdie pushed aside the screen door.

"Get in here this instant!" she snapped. "How could you be so inconsiderate, Memphis, running off like that, as if Naomi doesn't have enough to contend with! You understand me?"

I ducked past her into the blessed shock of cool air and headed for the sink. I gulped down two glasses of water, one right after the other, then leaned over the sink and splashed the tap water up into my face.

"Where have you been?" She was irritated with me and making no bones about it.

"Did Clover decide to give up and come on back, or are they still praying her in?" The words bubbled up out of me like regurgitated water. I thought I was being funny and laughed. Aunt Birdie just looked at me.

I was sweaty and dirty. My ponytail had unraveled, and I could feel my hair sticking out every which way. I could see the dust settled in the pores of my skin and the arcs of dirt underneath my fingernails.

"What are we going to do with you?" She cupped my chin in her hand, shook her head, and sighed. "No, Clover's not back." I'd never seen her so tired. "You look awful," she said. "Go on upstairs and get cleaned up."

"Did the sheriff come by?"

She stepped back at arm's length, a pucker between her eyebrows. "Is that what you're worried about? I'll be right here, O.K.? There's nothing to be afraid of. Now, get along."

The door to Clover's room was ajar. The shades were drawn, and the dim silence inside seemed mysterious. When I pushed the door wide open, a laundry-soap smell drifted out toward me. Someone had been in the room. Naomi, I guessed, before the prayer circle showed up.

Some of Clover's little boxes were on the bed, their lids off, their contents fingered. An empty cologne bottle. Carefully folded squares of chewing-gum foil. Three pale-as-bone pebbles. Oak leaves, perfectly dried. Faded wildflowers, giving off a dry, muted scent of old summers.

Then I recognized a piece of white paper askew in one of the boxes. It was my first report card from Blue Parrot Grade School, one of those things you don't even know you've lost until you accidentally find it again. I picked it up. My name was scratched out, and just above it, in labored block printing, was her name—Clover. Why would she do that? I stared at the card for a long time as my thoughts wandered into a vaguely hurting place. Then I put the card back in its box. I understood—clearly—that it didn't belong to me anymore.

In another box there was a snapshot of two tiny girls leaning through the donut hole of a tire swing that hung from the limb of a big tree. It was the oak in front of the house. The girls were squinting against the sun, their little legs entwined. It was so alive I could almost hear them giggling, could almost see the tire swaying. With a start, I realized I was looking at a childhood picture of my mother, Rosie, and her little sister, Clover. Seeing Rosie triggered the old familiar ache of homesickness for a life that would never come back.

I started to return the picture to its box, but the expression on Clover's little face stopped me. I looked closer. How old was she? Was it just before the meningitis changed her life forever? She was grinning with pure happiness at her big sister, the sister who'd grown up and left her and never looked back. I threw the picture down and fled to my room.

After my shower I flopped on the bed, wrung out from the strange, unsettling day. I could hear the prayer meeting breaking up downstairs. Mrs. Preacher Dalton called out, "Remember, we're holding you up in our prayers!" That was followed by the slamming of car doors and engines humming as they headed down the driveway.

All the day's pushing and pulling of feelings had left me off kilter. Everything was going by too fast, like one of those speeded-up old-time movies. The flat coolness from the big air conditioner downstairs had finally eased its way up to my room, and I closed my eyes, giving myself over to weariness.

Aunt Birdie shook me awake.

"Get up, honey. Wilson's downstairs." Wilson. The sheriff. She pulled a clean pair of shorts and a top from my dresser and chucked them onto the foot of the bed. "Slip these on. And straighten up your hair."

I pushed myself up on my elbows, groggy, a little disoriented. "Why do I . . ."

"Have to talk to him?" she finished. "Because it's his job." She looked at me, her mouth set. "Do you have any idea how many people are out there searching for Clover? No, I doubt it. You've been off gallivanting around."

She bent down, rummaging through the tumble of shoes and sandals on the closet floor. "The traffic on this road today—mercy! Folks from Oaklee and Abbotsville and from back up in the country, all driving in to help search." She matched up a pair of sandals and dropped them by the side of the bed. "The kudzu's so thick across the highway, Wilson's sent for Duke. Clover could be anywhere in there—hurt."

She stood at the foot of the bed, waiting, her folded arms cradling her full bosom. "Well? Get a move on!"

My mind hadn't gotten any farther than *Duke*. He was the most famous bloodhound in these parts. He'd tracked a little kidnapped girl to a cabin upcountry the year before. There was a picture of him with her and her folks on the front page of the big Sunday paper out of Charleston, along with an article about how his puppies were selling for big prices, one even going clear out to California. The Jackson County Sheriff's Department managed to get one of the puppies after churches all over held bake sales and picnic raffles to pay for it. But Nosy Lady—that's what they named her—was probably still too much a puppy to be on the job looking for anybody on her own.

I stood in front of the dresser mirror, smoothed back my hair, and reset my barrettes. I was flushed with sunburn. "My nose looks like a radish," I said, mostly to myself.

"Rub some lotion on your face and arms." Aunt Birdie glanced at her watch.

"Aunt Birdie, what should I tell him about that Old Roy?"

"Everything." She patted me on my shoulder and walked me out into the hallway. "Whatever he asks, just answer truthfully. We've got to find Clover and get her home before . . ."

As we headed down the stairs, a shadowy picture darted across my mind: the searchers pulling something dark and lifeless out of the swamp. I gripped Aunt Birdie's arm and tried to take a deep breath.

"It's O.K., honey," she said. "Don't be scared. Wilson and your grandpa Jeb were boys together. It's just routine."

But my stomach was doing somersaults. Sheriff Wilson was bound to be filled to the brim with Naomi's bad feelings about me.

He was standing at the mantel and turned toward the doorway when we came in. He was a big man with golden, weathered skin and thinning brown hair. When he moved, even slightly, all the dark, intimidating leather on him creaked—his heavy boots, his thick belt with little silver-colored ring hooks on it, his leather holster riding on another low-slung belt. It was the first time I'd seen him up close.

Aunt Birdie eased me to one end of the sofa and sat down next to me, holding my hand. "Sheriff," she said, "this is Memphis."

"Sorry we have to meet under these circumstances, Memphis." He leaned over, grabbed up my limp hand, and squeezed it. Then he sat down in the overstuffed tweed chair across the coffee table.

Naomi never took her eyes off me, rocking slowly in her platform chair, sitting back just far enough from the sofa so she was watching, not participating. She had deep shadows beneath her eyes, and her freckles were so stark against her slack, pale face they looked as though they'd been jabbed on with an eyebrow pencil. I tried to smile at her, but she gazed right through me. My lip stuck against my dry teeth, and I turned away.

Sheriff Wilson caught the exchange and gave me a kindly look. He leaned forward, resting his forearms against his knees, smelling of aftershave and baby powder.

"Memphis, we've got us a problem here, and you know what that is. Your aunt's missing, and we can't seem to find her. We've done a house-to-house check, and nobody's seen her since yesterday morning. Now, is there anything you can think of that might help us get her back home?" He gave me one of those helpless little smiles grownups are good at when they're setting traps.

I shook my head.

He studied his immaculate fingernails, then looked back up at me. "Why don't we talk about yesterday morning before she left? Did you have an argument?"

"Yes, sir."

"You two argue a lot, don't you?"

"Yes, sir."

"You ever fight? Like hit each other?"

"Hit each other? No."

"But you sometimes break things?" He glanced over at Naomi. She just kept rocking back and forth, staring at me, her hands folded in her lap.

"I don't break her stuff. She breaks mine."

"I bet that makes you pretty mad sometimes." There was that smile again.

"Wouldn't it make you mad?"

He almost smiled but looked away quickly, as if pulling his thoughts together. Then he glanced at Naomi again.

"Yes, I think it probably would . . . and I think I might even want to light into the person who broke my stuff."

All three of them were staring at me. So there it was. He was asking me if I'd done something to her—not in so many words, but that was it.

"I didn't hurt her," I said, hearing my voice rise. "She . . . she knew she went too far and she left."

Aunt Birdie started shifting around on the sofa the same way she'd fidgeted when Miss Ferguson came to the front porch that first year, talking about me and my rowdy ways.

"How far was *too* far, Memphis?" His green-speckled eyes searched my face, drawing me in.

"She broke my mother's guitar." There. She broke it. Period. I didn't have to tell them why it broke my heart. They wouldn't believe me anyway.

"Did she break it outright, or did you struggle for it, and it somehow got broken?"

"She broke it. She slammed it down on the edge of the dresser. Then she threw it at me and ran."

"Then what happened?"

"We ran down the stairs, and she slammed out the front door."

"Now, think carefully, Memphis. Did Clover actually run out the front door? Did you see her go out to the road?"

"Yes, she headed down toward Johnsons'."

"There's no doubt in your mind that you saw her . . ."

Aunt Birdie lurched forward. "Whoa!" she said. "Hold up, Wilson! This is sounding like the third degree or whatever you call it!" She looked over at Naomi. "This is off base."

"Calm down, Miss Birdie," said Wilson. "We're strictly off the record here. Just trying to get the lay of the land. Miss Naomi gave me to understand there was a lot of bad feeling between these two."

"Well, this girl is not capable of whatever it is you're edging toward!" She settled back beside me.

Sheriff Wilson nodded agreeably. "You live down the road, don't you, Miss Birdie? You saw Clover pass by yesterday morning?"

"Well, no, I was cold-packing tomatoes in the kitchen."

"I got this awful feeling in the pit of my stomach." Naomi's words were raspy and hard as little dry rocks. "I can't help but think Memphis might've . . ."

"Stop it," said Aunt Birdie, grabbing my hand and holding it tight.

Naomi didn't even hear her. "She's always just standing around studying everything. Who knows what's going on inside her head? Do you know how many times I catch her looking at me with that damned Riley expression on her face?" Her eyes seemed to bore right through my head, and I heard a small voice deep inside whisper, *Better run.*

Sheriff Wilson raised one hand and tried to say something, but Aunt Birdie jumped in before he could get a word out.

"Naomi, stop it! Can't you see what you're doing?"

"She was sneaky enough to get up to the attic and steal that damned guitar! She's a spiteful girl who goes out of her way to keep Clover in turmoil!" Naomi's sudden anger was pumping blood back up into her face. "And why was it all busted up anyway? Clover doesn't just break things for the hell of it!" Her voice cracked. "Damn that John Riley! First he steals Rosie, then his kid turns this house into a battlefield!" She glared at me, her front teeth biting at her lower lip as though trying to scrape the angry words loose.

"Merciful God, Naomi, she's Rosie's child, too!"

"Oh, you're really sure about that? She doesn't look like my side of the family, and I don't see anything Martin there, either. Look at her, already a foot taller than Clover and me. And that hair! Nobody in my family ever had a mess like that!"

Her eyes swept across the mantel that held her wedding portrait at one end and, at the other, a picture of her husband taken six months before the train accident that killed him. Hanging against the blue-flowered wallpaper above were fading tintypes of long-dead family, all watching us with steady, unamused eyes.

"No birth certificate! No nothing! How do I know she's Rosie's child?"

I felt my body go rigid.

Naomi's eyes were glassy, and I realized she'd fortified herself with blackberry wine.

Aunt Birdie gasped, put her arm around me, and drew me close. "Naomi doesn't mean this, Wilson." Her voice quavered. "She's so afraid and upset, she's not thinking straight."

Sheriff Wilson didn't seem too fazed. I guess he'd seen a lot of human nature at work. He shook his head, almost sadly, then got to his feet. I saw a look of understanding pass between him and Aunt Birdie.

"Memphis, Miss Birdie tells me there was a transient around here this morning. Why don't we step out on the porch and talk about it."

Outside, he asked me lots of questions about the old guy—what he looked like, what he'd said, what time he'd shown up, those kinds of things. He said he knew who Old Roy was and would alert his deputies to be on the lookout for him. He said I might have to make a face-to-face identification and asked if that would scare me. I told him maybe. Then he asked me not to be wandering off until this thing got settled. He said times were changing and not always for the best.

He started down the porch steps, then paused and looked back at me. "Actually," he said, "you're the spitting image of your grandpa Martin."

I watched him cross the yard to his cruiser, a big, hefty, solid man. He reminded me a little bit of Samson's daddy. There was something about real daddies, something I knew but couldn't quite put my finger on. I wanted to run after him and tell him that once upon a time John Riley had tried to be a real daddy, too—but I didn't.

He gave me a little two-finger salute off the side of his forehead just as he headed his cruiser down the driveway.

9

I sat out on the porch for a long time after Sheriff Wilson left. Naomi had cut me to the bone, leaving no doubt as to where I stood with her. But instead of being full of rage, I was flat, numbed out. Talking with Wilson had helped. He'd been kind, and I hoped he wasn't just feeling sorry for me—I hoped I really did remind him of my grandpa Martin.

I tried to imagine Wilson and my grandfather as boys, leaving their fingerprints on the same trees and rocks Samson and I touched, walking through the same meadows ringed with the same pines, smelling the same old stink of Moody Bog.

Twilight crept in, scattering a pearly glow over the trees and yard. Fireflies flitted out from the rose-entwined wisteria, and the chickens out back clucked softly as they settled down for the night. I pushed my legs out and gave the swing a little start with my toes.

Through the peeking space between the sheer lace panels at the living room window, I could see Naomi and

Aunt Birdie. Except for showering, things like that, they'd been together steadily since Clover disappeared. When either of them slept was anybody's guess. And nobody was doing a lot of eating. Aunt Birdie even asked Samson to stop by and feed her sweet old cat, Fannie. As I studied them, Naomi got up from her rocker, her face frozen in a scowl. She eased herself onto the sofa, kicked off her sandals, and stretched out on her back with the phone positioned atop her stomach. She seemed older, her movements stiff and lingering. Aunt Birdie glanced toward the window and saw me. Then she got up, turned on the television, and settled down in the big tweed chair.

They seemed so comfortable with each other, and I thought maybe that's what sisters are supposed to be like. They probably knew everything there was to know about each other—Blue Parrot wasn't a place for secrets. They didn't agree on everything, certainly not on me, but you could tell they loved each other and probably always would.

I understood why Naomi loved Aunt Birdie. Everybody loved her. But I couldn't understand how Aunt Birdie could love someone like Naomi Martin.

Naomi's words sat cold and leaden inside my brain: *nobody in my family ever looked like that.* She'd never raised her hand to me. She'd simply withheld herself. She didn't want me around and didn't know how to get rid of me. What had she said? I'd turned her house into a battlefield? As if it was a one-sided thing I'd done deliberately. I wanted to close my eyes and never have to see all this again.

As the deepening purple shadows settled over the yard, I could just make out a thin black-and-white field cat moving furtively along the blackberry bushes. It paused, listened, and disappeared in and out of the shadows. Hungry, I knew, and always on the prowl. Did it ever see big marmalade Fannie in all her feline, pampered glory basking in Aunt Birdie's front window?

Who decides what life we get, anyway? Swirling in over the threadbare sorrow inside my head came a sound, plaintive as the call of a mourning dove. But it wasn't my pain I heard. It was Clover's. She was out there— somewhere.

About midnight, a silence settled over the house, so powerful it woke me. I sat up in bed, listening. The lumbering drone of the air conditioner was missing. It was out again. It was old and tired and had been patched up, slapped on the rump, and sent back in to play too many times. Gradually a faint, fitful snoring drifted up from downstairs. I recognized it and was surprised at how glad I felt that Naomi was sleeping. The soft, sliding slap of bare feet on wood came along the hallway, traveled up the steps, and stopped at my door.

Aunt Birdie stood there in her slip, her yellow hair undone and curling on her shoulders. A spill of moonlight through the window lit her face, erasing the years.

"Aunt Birdie?" I rubbed my eyes.

"Did I wake you?" She sat on the side of the bed, her light, familiar scent sweetening the air between us. "I been worrying about you."

"The air conditioner went out again," I said.

There was a pause.

"About tonight . . ."

"Please, Aunt Birdie, don't. I don't want to hear it. She said it all."

"She didn't mean it, honey. I know she didn't. You do, too, don't you?"

"She said it. Out loud. In front of you. And in front of Sheriff Wilson."

"Maybe you have to be the forgiving one here, Memphis."

"Why? Because Clover's missing, she can say anything? And I'm not supposed to mind?"

"Because she's hurting in a way you can't understand."

"Maybe I'm hurting in a way she can't understand." I drew my knees up and hugged them close.

"You think I don't know that?"

"Sheriff Wilson said I looked just like Grandpa Martin."

"You do. You absolutely do. You're as beautiful a girl as he was handsome." A huskiness crept into her voice.

On an impulse I asked, "Did you love my grandpa, Aunt Birdie?"

"Oh yes. He was a very easy person to love."

"No, I mean, did you *love* him?"

She lost herself in thought then, as though dipping into a long-quiet stream of memories. I knew if we were sitting on the porch in broad daylight, we wouldn't be having this conversation. This shadowy room streaked with moonlight had tripped a latch.

"Oh, that was all so long ago," she said finally. "He's dead and gone, bless his sweet heart."

We were silent for a while, and my mind stumbled around a puzzle that wasn't in my power to figure out.

"You should've been my grandmama." I reached out and touched her arm as though that would somehow make it so.

She stood up, lifting her hair off her neck, then letting it fall back.

"Should've doesn't count, honey. That's all water under the bridge now anyway, isn't it?" She walked to the window and stared out across the night. "Your grandmama is a tough woman. She's been through a lot, but if anything bad's happened to Clover, she'll go down hard. You understand?" She turned and headed for the door. "Let's try to catch a few more winks. The dog handler will be here in the morning. God willing . . ."

Her sigh fluttered up and drifted across the room like a prayer on nervous midnight wings.

"Aunt Birdie?"

"Yes?" She turned in the moonlight and looked back at me.

"About Clover . . . I need to tell you something."

"Yes?"

"I told her I wished she was dead." The shame of those words seemed to burn my tongue.

She was motionless for a moment, then, very carefully, she said, "We all say things we don't mean."

"But I'm scared," I said.

"We're all scared, Memphis. If it'll make you feel better, say a prayer for her."

I was trapped inside a terrible dream, scrambling to get out. A boiling yellow sky bruised with purple clouds glowered overhead, and in the streets below, houses with locked doors and unlit windows shuddered and groaned as I raced by. Naomi looked at me from an upstairs window, and when I banged on the front door, she slammed the window shut.

Something dark was chasing me, something treacherous as the murky waters of Moody Bog, two-headed, with snapping teeth and a rage like Judgment Day. Off in the distance, Lady Althea rose up out of a mound of blood-red rocks. She pointed her finger at me, and her voice cracked like thunder across the furious sky: *A terrible burden! A terrible burden!* She swung a bullwhip snake above her head, and as she brought it down in front of her with a mighty howl, it turned into an avenging sword, and then Old Roy's head came rolling down the street, grinning and winking. I screamed, and Sheriff Wilson pointed up at John Riley as he flew by overhead, searching for me with blind Orphan-Annie eyes.

Just as I spun toward unbearable panic, the nightmare spit me out. I opened my eyes to a hazy daylight filtering through the windows of my room.

As far back as I can remember, I've been a dream traveler—sometimes soaring across enchanted azure skies and sometimes plunging into an abyss. But Rosie taught me early on how to ground my waking mind.

When I was around three or four, I went through a strange siege of wild dreams—of old-time sailing ships bucking and rolling through heavy squalls, of great gray whales fighting for their lives, leaving wide trails of blood in the water. I'd wake up sobbing, and Rosie would hug me close and tell me it was just my soul talking to me. Then she'd look into my face and say, "You know what's important? Today, that's what, right here and now." Then she'd ask me, "What day is today, baby?"

Rosie—I'd already figured out that I'd be missing her for the rest of my life. We spent our last day together in the little park on the second corner down from our apartment. It was spring in New Orleans—May, I think. I was seven and in love with the rowdy birds that flashed back and forth through the spreading oak trees. Our landlord, Archie, gave me a sack of stale breadcrumbs to lure them down. Rosie let go of my hand so I could race ahead while John Riley stopped at a vendor to buy us a dinner of hot dogs. I heard her call out, "Look how the birds love Memphis!" Then I heard someone else say, "Oh my God." I turned and saw Rosie crumpled on the green grass. I thought she was playing one of her teasing games, a trick. A patrol car pulled to the curb, and a woman on the sidewalk pointed toward me. John Riley came running across the park to Rosie, then looked around for me. Just as he reached me, the hot dogs slid out of their paper wrappers to the ground. Two scrawny dogs sprang from the bushes and snatched them up. I was hungry and hollered at them. I didn't know my mother was dead.

I slipped from bed and padded to the window. The growing day outside was misty, translucent; its sun glowed like a promise behind a pale, cloudless sky. I thought I heard Rosie whisper, "What day is *today*, Memphis?"

This is the day the famous bloodhound comes to Blue Parrot.

10

Fifteen minutes later, in clean shorts and shirt, hair brushed and pulled back in a ponytail, I sat on the top step of the landing, trying to figure out exactly what to say, how to act when I went downstairs. I could hear Naomi and Aunt Birdie in the kitchen, talking between themselves as they drank their coffee.

Aunt Birdie said, "Well, that was Ida Avery who called earlier. Everybody's gathering at the church to put their prayers behind Hollister and his mission, all day if need be. Might be a good idea for us to be there, too, you think?"

"We'll see," said Naomi.

"Maybe you shouldn't be here, just sitting around, waiting God knows how long. That's all I'm thinking."

"I said we'll see, Bird."

They sounded calm enough. I knew I had to face Naomi, so I tried to set a mild expression on my face and made my way downstairs to the kitchen. Naomi didn't even look up. I felt awkward, as though my arms and legs might suddenly flail about in any direction without warning. I smiled at Aunt Birdie and moved around quietly, making myself a piece of peanut-butter toast and pouring a glass of orange juice. I stood at the counter, not quite sure if I should sit at the table.

Aunt Birdie patted the empty chair next to her. "Sit down, honey. There's some news about that Old Roy."

Naomi moved her cup back and forth over the vinyl tablecloth, still not looking at me.

"Bowen stopped by earlier and said they picked him up about four o'clock this morning, trying to jimmy the back door of the drug store. While they were booking him at Oaklee, they found Clover's cap in his back pocket. He says he found it up by the turnoff."

"I hope that man didn't hurt my girl." Naomi's voice was tight, razor sharp. I glanced at her just in time to catch her eye before she looked back down at the table.

The telephone finally broke the painful silence.

Naomi grabbed the receiver up to her ear. She told Aunt Birdie it was Sheriff Wilson, then mostly listened.

"Hollister's going to be here around ten," she said when she hung up. Hollister was Duke's handler, and just the thought of somebody famous showing up in Blue Parrot—even if it was a bloodhound—was exciting. I could hardly wait to tell Samson.

"Wilson said there's a couple of things we need to know about how they get a good track."

Aunt Birdie and I leaned toward her.

"Hollister won't bring the dog up to the house—something about the family scent." She stopped and took a deep breath. "He needs a piece of Clover's clothing or something like her pillowcase. And they have to shut down traffic on the road so the car fumes don't mess up the trail." Her face clouded, and her chin trembled slightly. "He said this is a good day for tracking, kind of overcast. Even rainy is good. Makes the scent rise up off the grass or something." Her head slumped forward. "Oh God, Birdie!" Her voice pitched up, sounding as though she could let out a scream that would make our hair stand on end.

Aunt Birdie reached over and stroked her arm. "It's all right, honey. Just hold on."

Naomi's words began running up so fast on each other they were hard to understand. "He said searchers are usually looking for footprints and things and can walk right by a person in heavy brush, but the dog's tracking a scent, nothing else, and won't quit, and he said I need to keep my spirits up, that Duke's the best there is. . . . Oh God, Birdie, you're right. I can't sit here waiting like this while some dog looks for my daughter." She jammed her face into her hands as if trying to suffocate her anxiety.

Aunt Birdie turned to me and shook her head. "We'll go down to the church," she murmured. She looked so tired, rumpled, and worried that I wanted to reach out and comfort her somehow as she'd so often done for me. "You know what to do when Hollister gets here, don't you?"

I nodded nervously and liked the thought of doing something to help.

Hollister showed up about an hour after they were gone. He looked like an old movie cowboy, tall and lanky with a lined face and big, bony hands. I'd been jittery waiting for him, watching the hands of the clock on the mantel and fumbling to the front window every five minutes. I gave Samson the news about Duke and had hardly hung up the phone before he was at the back door. Now we stood looking up at Hollister with awe—a real live tracker. We craned our necks, trying to see around him to wherever his famous bloodhound was. I guess Hollister was used to the attention, because his faded blue eyes looked as if they were smiling, even though his mouth wasn't.

"I haven't let him out yet," he said. "Is Mrs. Martin ready with the garment?"

"She's down at the church," I said, "but I've got the pillowcase right here." I grabbed it off the arm of the sofa and handed it to him.

He nodded politely. "Y'all stay put up here," he said. "Don't come down to the road. You can see Duke from your porch. I'll be exercising him for a few minutes before we get to work."

"Yes, sir!" We followed him across the porch, stopping at the steps, and watched him lope down the driveway to his station wagon. He even walked like a movie cowboy.

"Wow," Samson said under his breath.

We eyed each other, then raced for the oak. From up in its towering crown, we could see across the open fields, up and down the highway, and even most of Blue Parrot behind us.

Hollister lifted up the station wagon's hatch, leaned in, then stepped aside as Duke hopped out. The dog stretched and shook himself out. He was wearing a leather harness, and Hollister had him on a long leash tethered to the wagon's tailgate. He was the color of honey, and Samson said he must have weighed more than a hundred pounds.

His head, with its folds of loose skin and long flapping ears, seemed too large for his powerful body.

"Look at his dome," Samson whispered.

"His what?"

"The top of his head. Where the brains are. Wow, he must have a ton."

Hollister gave him some fresh water and walked him over to a tree to let him relieve himself. Then they trotted back and forth across the front of the yard a few times.

I knew the instant they were about to start. There was something in their manner with each other, as if they'd cleared their throats, straightened their shoulders. Hollister got the pillowcase and fluffed it under Duke's nose, then laid it on the ground. Duke examined it, his long ears just about hiding it from sight. Then he lifted his head, nose up, and trotted out onto Blue Parrot Road. He circled slowly before heading down toward town. A few feet down the road, it was as if a charge of electricity shot through him. His tail went up, and he veered off into the vacant field, picking up speed so quickly the slack went out of his lead. Hollister broke into giant strides to keep up with him.

"Wow!" Samson's voice quivered with excitement. "That's one powerful dog!" He glanced at me. "What's the matter?"

"They're heading straight across the field for the highway," I said. "That Old Roy, he told me he'd been sleeping up there. He was joking about all the kudzu."

We got very quiet. In all our excitement about this big famous dog, we'd forgotten what he might find. We were perched up in the tree, watching as though it was a sideshow or something.

Across the field, Hollister and Duke reached the thick kudzu hedge that bordered the highway. They stood still for a moment, then Hollister followed Duke back and forth along the hedge—back and forth, back and forth, as though Duke couldn't make up his mind.

Several deputies stood next to the cruisers that blocked the highway a few yards on either side of where Duke was working. Traffic was beginning to back up north and south, and some people were getting out of their cars and walking up to the cruiser barricade for a look at whatever was going on. The deputies were motioning them to stay back.

I recognized the tall, hefty man who got out of one of the cruisers and walked down the highway to Hollister. It was Sheriff Wilson. They stood together, then Hollister pointed across the road, and they seemed to agree on something. Wilson walked back and leaned against his cruiser, and Hollister and Duke backtracked along the hedge to Blue Parrot Road, then turned out onto the main highway. Just that quick, Duke's tail stood up on alert again, and they went straight into the heavy brush on the other side. A couple of deputies with machetes ran down and followed them in.

"Wow!" Samson pushed his hair back off his forehead. His eyes were shining, and his mouth was open. "If she's in there," he said, "that dog's gonna find her!"

"Sam, am I to blame for this?" I had to know what he thought.

"What?" His clear gaze was steady, unwavering.

"I said some rotten things to her. Do you think it could have started some kind of chain reaction, like it got loose in the air, and something . . ."

"Naw." He said it too quickly, then reached over and took my hand and squeezed it.

It was the first time he'd ever touched me out of the blue like that. I didn't know what to do. He seemed so close, closer than he'd ever been. His T-shirt carried wispy scents of dogs and weeds and garden soil—and the vaguely unsettling odor of his boy's body. I felt a warmth creep up over me, whispering along my arms and neck and slipping into my brain.

He leaned over and kissed me, his lips soft as butterfly wings against my own. His breath, flowing over my face, was sweet with the scent of cinnamon. It's hard to say which of us was more surprised.

Later we tried to pretend it didn't make a difference. But an unfamiliar shyness had crept in, and I had a sudden lonesome feeling that our days of roaming the back fields and swamplands of Blue Parrot alone together were over.

11

For the first time in a long while, I thought of my John Riley marker up by the highway and wondered if it was still there, if Sheriff Wilson had seen it.

When Samson and I first started running puppy-wild through the fields of Blue Parrot together, we discovered that people on their way to Florida often threw stuff from their cars. Every Saturday, rain or shine, we made our way up to the ditch alongside the highway and walked the length of it, from behind Johnson's General Store down past the Blue Parrot Road turnoff. There were always food wrappers and cigarette stubs and empty bottles. We found lots of trash—sunglasses with one ear stem broken off, magazines, torn-up snapshots of goofy-looking people that we sometimes spent hours piecing together. Every once in a while there was a pair of sandals or even underwear, and one time we found a big bag of chocolate cookies that we were going to eat until we saw bugs crawling around inside.

The worst thing we ever found was a sack of kittens, all of them dead but one. Samson tried for a week to keep the last one alive, but it didn't make it. The most thrilling thing was a gun with a silver-and-pearl handle. Samson took it home to his daddy, who just about fainted when he saw it was loaded. He said it might have been used to commit a crime and turned it over to old Deputy Crowder. Then there was a little red plastic radio, cracked on one side, that Naomi let me hook up out in the henhouse to keep the chickens company.

Samson and I found the place for my John Riley marker one Saturday when we flopped under the big pecan tree that shaded the far side of the turnoff.

I saw something glinting in the yellow grass.

"It might be some kind of treasure," I said.

It was a rusting oil can. Curled next to it was what we first thought was a small black snake, but it turned out to be a broken engine belt. We handed the things back and forth, turning them over and around, looking for clues and signs.

"This stuff is really old," Samson said, sliding his fingertips over the can.

"You know what I think?" I asked. "I think I was meant to find it. I think this is where John Riley's VW broke down." I searched his face to see if he agreed. He seemed impressed.

The next morning we went back up to the place with one of my troll dolls and planted its feet in the dirt, then propped the oil can and frayed belt behind it. I ringed the whole thing with pebbles to set it off.

"Do you think John Riley could see this if he drove by?"

Samson looked skeptical but nodded anyway.

"Well," I said, "I think he could."

But suppose John Riley's bus hadn't broken down where and when it did? Then he'd never have met Rosie. She'd have never run off with him. Just a few more miles down the road, and there wouldn't have been any Memphis Riley. I'd have been somebody else. Maybe with perfect, straight black hair that lay back from my face like raven wings. Maybe living in Jacksonville or Miami in a big pink apartment building fronted by a long winding beach, spending my afternoons going to the movies and eating cherry snow cones whenever I wanted. Who decided I'd be me and not that girl?

The wall phone rang. My hand shook as I put the receiver to my ear. Oh Lord, I thought, it's gonna be bad news about Clover.

"Memphis?"

"Aunt Birdie—hey."

"You O.K.? You sound funny."

I could still feel Samson's lips. And I could still see Hollister and Duke plunging into the thick brush across the highway. I could still smell Samson's cinnamon breath. And I could still see Sheriff Wilson leaning against his cruiser, waiting.

"Memphis? Is anything wrong?"

"I'm just . . . I don't know. I'm O.K. They're looking on the other side of the highway."

"You went up there?"

"Samson and I were up in the oak. We could see it all."

Samson. The same, but different now. Afterward I'd watched him skirt alongside the blackberry bushes as he always did and cut across Aunt Birdie's property. But he was different now. I'd waited to see if he would look back. He didn't.

"Aunt Birdie, do you know where the guitar is?"

She paused. "Yes. It's on the shelf under the sink. Why?"

"No reason."

"How long ago did they go across the highway?" she asked.

"A half hour maybe." I'd never ever thought of kissing Samson—and now I couldn't get the scent of him out of my mind.

"Well, I called Wilson's dispatcher to let him know where Naomi is—in case . . ."

In case. After she hung up, the words dangled in front of me, loose and winking with meaning. *In case she's alive. In case she's not.* My jittery insides seemed to push little thorns through my skin all along my arms, my neck, over my shoulders, prickling across my scalp. Everything was out of control. Changing.

I stooped down and pulled the mangled guitar from under the sink. Even crippled, it seemed to leap into my arms, its twisted strings full of a soft buzz. I cradled it close and carried it gently as I would a baby out to the swing on the front porch. And the word that Rosie had never taught me—*mama*—whispered up out of my throat as I swayed back and forth.

It's your sister, your baby sister, they're looking for, Mama, my Rosie Mama . . . the one you ran away from. What do I do . . . in case, Mama? What if terrible Old Roy hurt her, maybe even killed her? What do I do, Mama? I didn't mean it when I wished she was dead. I just wanted to keep what was mine. If I'd let her have your guitar, maybe none of this would have happened. She'd be home now, right this very minute— driving me crazy, but alive. And I could do better, be better. I'd hand her the guitar, even if it broke my heart. If she never comes home again, Mama, Naomi will hate me worse than ever. And if Naomi can never stand the sight of me, where do I go? Can't you find Clover and somehow show her the way home? Can't you find John Riley and tell him I need him now worse than ever? Everything and everybody is out of wack here, Rosie. Out of wack, my Rosie Mama.

I sighed and looked out across the front yard. The morning's overcast was lifting, and the sun's muted yellow face, glowing behind the skin of the sky, warmed the air.

I wanted to put everything back the way it was three days ago. I wanted Clover home, scrubbing and dusting and even glaring at me. I wanted Samson back. The old Samson. I wanted to run down the road, catch him out in his front yard, and punch him as hard as I could. I'd make him take the kiss back, make him put things back the way they were. But you can't take back one second of your life. It just moves on to the next and the one after that, on and on for as long as you live.

A distant howl—Duke's howl—arced over the sky on the wings of a red-tailed hawk. It soared up across the glowing sun, then turned, swooped down, and boomeranged back across the highway.

What had seemed a haunting, waiting stillness just moments earlier now shattered like an eggshell. The excited voices of the men on the highway carried across the field. A car engine coughed, then roared, and I ran to the steps, stretching to see. A cruiser came flying down the road into Blue Parrot. It was Sheriff Wilson. I waved frantically, but he didn't see me. I willed my suddenly leaden legs to take me down the steps and across the yard to the road.

Off in the distance, coming from Oaklee, was the frightening scream of a siren. I pushed myself forward harder and harder, finally racing, my heart pounding, my breath balled up in my throat.

Please God, don't let it be anything bad. Let her be alive. Please. I'll do anything You want. I'll be good. I'll change, I promise. For the rest of my life, I'll be good. Please.

Then I was at the highway, the shrieking siren rushing toward me, hurting my ears, filling up my head. Down the road I could see people scrambling out of their cars, some even clambering atop to get a better look. The deputies milled about uneasily, as though they weren't quite sure what to expect next. The siren cut suddenly. An ambulance slowed and slid to a stop on the other side of the road, its red running lights still flashing.

I started to dash across the highway, but a hand gripped my wrist and pulled me back. It was Deputy Bowen standing right next to me, and I hadn't even seen him.

"I've got to go over there," I cried.

"No," he said, shaking his head. "You can't."

"I've got to see!" I tried to jerk my arm away, but he wouldn't let go.

"No," he said. "We'll wait here."

We heard the brush crackling and the voices, urgent and strident, lifting up into the air and fading before lifting up again. The medics jumped from the ambulance, leaving its front doors flapped open like wings. They rushed around back and jerked the rear doors open. They slid out a stretcher, popped its legs down, and rolled it around to the side, hidden from view.

"No!" I cried. "I have to see!" I knew enough from watching *Hawaii Five-O* that if they pulled a sheet over her face, she was—not alive. I had to know. But Bowen held me fast. I twisted around to kick him, but he sidestepped, and I wound up trying to butt him in the stomach with my head. Suddenly I was off the ground, my legs dangling.

"Stop it!" he said, jerking me hard. "Just stop it, girl!"

We heard the ambulance doors slam. *Bam. Bam. Bam. Bam.* All four. She was inside.

Bowen lowered me to the ground as the ambulance made a U-turn to head back to Oaklee. Flying up Blue Parrot Road was Sheriff Wilson's cruiser. It cut onto the highway and pulled in behind the ambulance. Naomi and Aunt Birdie were in the backseat. Naomi was staring straight ahead, her face clean as a slate, as though all her features had been erased. As the cruiser passed us, Aunt Birdie's stricken eyes glanced our way, but she didn't see me. The sirens suddenly blared, and Bowen lurched in surprise. I jerked loose and ran down the highway after them.

"Wait!" I yelled. "Wait! Aunt Birdie, wait!" The distance between us widened as they sped off. Deputy Bowen came up behind me, panting to catch his breath.

"Come on, Memphis," he said. "You shouldn't be by yourself. Maybe you oughta . . ."

"No," I said. "Just take me back to the house."

I sat out on the back steps with the kitchen door wide open so I could hear the phone if it rang.

"Memphis?" It was Samson's mama, Gina.

I hadn't heard any cars pull up and wondered if she'd walked all the way from her place.

"Deputy Bowen told me you were here by yourself." She walked over and leaned her elbow on the porch rail. She was short but not light-boned like Naomi and Clover. She looked strong, with wide hips and solid legs. Her brown eyes gazed out at me with concern as she brushed back flyaway strands of graying hair from her face. "Won't you come down and have supper with us?"

I shook my head. I didn't want to be anywhere near Samson.

"You really shouldn't be alone right now." She eased over so gently I hardly knew she was moving and sat next to me. Her voice still carried strong traces of New Jersey, always reminding me of John Riley's rat-a-tat, musical voice.

"I'm O.K.," I said, staring down at my dusty feet and the scruffy sandals I'd kicked off.

She leaned forward, resting her forearms on her knees and lacing her fingers together. I cut my eyes over at her face. She was gazing straight ahead, staring at something inside her mind.

"You know," she said after a while, "when I was five, I ran out into the street after a ball. My cousin, Frannie, dashed off the stoop and grabbed me out of the path of a truck and threw me up on the curb. But she got hit. She was only nine. She's been in a wheelchair ever since." Her voice was soft and steady. "It took me years and years to come to terms with that. And you know, the funny thing is, in my dreams, my prayers for a miracle always come true. In my dreams, Frannie runs and jumps and . . ." She looked at me, a rueful smile caught at the corners of her mouth, her thick eyebrows lifted winglike above her sympathetic eyes.

I knew she was trying to reach the pain inside me. For an instant, just an instant, I wanted to lean my head on her shoulder and feel her strong, motherly arms around me.

She stood up, and I felt her hand move lightly over the top of my head. "I wish you'd come down for supper," she said. "It doesn't feel right leaving you here alone."

"I'm O.K.," I said again. "The prayer circle brought lots of food."

"You want me to stay here with you until . . ."

"No," I said quickly. I wanted to be by myself. I wanted to spread out on my bed, close my eyes, and disappear.

"If you change your mind . . ."

I nodded.

"You'll call if you . . ."

"Yes."

But I knew I wouldn't change my mind. The last thing I wanted was to be sitting across the table from Samson, trying to pretend that what had happened up in the tree hadn't really happened.

"Mrs. Greeley?" I called after her, before she turned the corner of the house.

She stopped instantly and looked back. Her homely face lit up with expectation, and I saw for the first time how beautiful she was.

"Thank you, ma'am," I said, surprising myself. The gratitude had come up and out all by itself, from the heart. From my muddled, weary heart.

12

The TV screen flickered in the corner. I sat up, shaking loose the numb weariness of waiting. After Gina Greeley left, I'd gone inside and prowled like a field cat through the house. Upstairs. Downstairs. Listening to every sound out on the road. Staring at the silent phone on the lamp table. Finally flopping on the sofa.

The familiar voice of Les Trent, the television announcer, buzzed up in my ears. There on the screen was Clover's face. Was he getting ready to say she was dead? I gripped the edge of the sofa cushion and heard the words coming straight toward me:

> Down state—the family of twenty-nine-year-old Blue Parrot resident Clover Martin is resting easier tonight. The Jackson County Sheriff's Office reports that tracking expert Wyman Hollister and his famed bloodhound, Duke, found Martin semiconscious and severely dehydrated in heavy brush about a mile and a half from where she disappeared last Tuesday morning. She was taken by

ambulance to Jackson County Hospital in
Oaklee. Sheriff Cooper Wilson's office is
investigating.

The opaque words spun off-kilter in the air in front of
me before slowly seeping in. She was in the hospital.
Alive. How much alive? Had Old Roy hurt her?

"Honey?" Aunt Birdie's voice startled me. She came
into the room and threw herself like a rag doll onto the
tweed chair. She'd lost weight. The lines at her mouth and
the corners of her eyes had deepened, and blue, crescent-
shaped shadows cupped the puffy skin beneath her tired
eyes.

"She's alive," I said, "in the hospital."

"Oh my lord, honey, you didn't know?" She pulled
herself forward in the chair.

"How would I know? Nobody bothered to tell me."

"I tried to call you a couple of times, honey, but the line
was busy. Then Bowen said he'd check in with you . . ."

"Well, he didn't! And the line wasn't busy—the phone
didn't ring once!" I was immediately sorry for snapping at
her and tried to do what she always did—glide on past the
rough spot. "Is she O.K.?"

"She will be. Course the mosquitoes got to her
something awful, and she lost a lot of weight. Looks like a
little toothpick."

"Did that Old Roy hurt her?"

She sighed and leaned back in the chair, rubbing one
elbow. "As much as they can piece together, she went off
across that field and came right up on him." She sucked
her breath in and shook her head. "Anyway, he scared the
daylights out of her, and she took off running. Instead of

heading back to the house, she ran toward the highway. Wilson said Roy doubled up laughing, telling him how Clover almost got hit by a car. I guess she just kept going and somehow got through all that tangle on the other side."

"Well, did she fall and hit her head or something? Why didn't she just start hollering?"

A sheen of tears filmed her eyes. "Hollister said they found her curled up in a ditch, covered with leaves—like she'd burrowed in there—and that's how they carried her out, all the way to the hospital, balled up, hard as a rock, with her eyes clenched shut. And she wouldn't open them until she heard Naomi's voice."

Yes, that would be Clover. Scared out of her wits when darkness fell. Darkness, with all its night creatures slithering, creeping, easing out cautiously to explore the new, frightened thing in their territory. I thought how scared I'd be, even knowing to holler, even knowing that somebody would find me sooner or later. But Clover? All she'd know was that she was alone in the dark. It figured that she'd burrow under leaves in a ditch.

"Oh God, Aunt Birdie, I didn't mean for all this to happen." No tears rushed up to ease the pain.

She was at my side, sitting next to me, holding me. "Of course you didn't. You think I don't know that?" She put her arms around me and rocked back and forth. "It's all right, honey. Everything's all right."

My thoughts were going wild, balling up into knots of doubt. I couldn't see how anything was all right for me. For Clover, maybe. She'd be back home with Naomi. Safe again. But me? I was worse off than ever, wasn't I? Naomi had finally let her true feelings out, and there was no going back. How was I going to live like that?

After a few minutes, Aunt Birdie patted my shoulder. "Let's rustle up a bite to eat and see if we can't just relax and thank God this thing is over."

I followed her out to the kitchen and flushed with embarrassment when I saw the wall phone's receiver dangling at the end of its cord. Sonny Rayburn had called earlier in the day, trying to disguise his voice, and told me to leave ten dollars down in the mailbox if I wanted to see Miss Clover alive. I'd yelled at him and must have missed the hook when I slammed the receiver down. Aunt Birdie didn't say a word as she settled it back on the hook.

We made our supper of ham-and-pickle sandwiches and lemonade. She sighed happily after she drained the last drop from her glass.

"That's the first food I've enjoyed since this thing happened." When I didn't answer, she said, "It's been awful for you, hasn't it?"

"Where's Naomi?" I asked.

"She's staying at the hospital. Everybody agreed Clover'd probably bounce back quicker if Naomi was there with her."

"I was wondering . . ."

"H'm?"

I couldn't get what I really wanted to say to come out of my mouth—the words of doubt and worry about how I fit in anymore, how I was supposed to act when Clover came home. My mind stumbled around, looking for a place to light, and up popped Old Roy's awful face. What about him, anyway?

"I was wondering—how people get to be like that Old Roy."

"You never know about people, honey. Seems he grew up around Branch Water, then went off to the war, the South Pacific, when he was only eighteen."

"Like Mr. Greeley?"

"No, this would be World War II. Let's see, the war ended in '45. This is '73, so that's . . ." She paused, doing the subtraction in her head. "Why that's twenty-eight years ago already! That makes him about . . ." Her eyes popped wide. "My God, that old wreck isn't even fifty! Can that be right? I thought he was *old!*"

Both Naomi and Aunt Birdie were in their fifties, but Aunt Birdie was always saying how she was still eighteen up in her head.

"Anyway, he spent time in one of those prisoner-of-war camps and went round the bend, I reckon. That war ate up a lot of good boys. Afterward he hit bottom—stealing, threatening people. Been in and out of jails and mental hospitals so much Wilson said even his own kinfolk are scared to death of him."

"You think he's hurt people?"

"Very likely." She pursed her lips, thinking about that. "Maybe it's a good thing Clover ran as hard as she did, even if it was the wrong way."

"What'll happen to him now?"

"Maybe they'll put him away for good. Let's hope, anyway. You have to wonder why they keep letting such a menace out. Life is one strange proposition sometimes." She pushed her chair back and stood up. "Let's call it a day, honey. I'm all done in. Naomi needs me to pack up a few things and take them in to her tomorrow morning."

I looked up at her. "What should I say when I see Clover?"

Her face clouded, and for a moment I thought it was going to crumble right off onto the floor. She rested her hands atop the chair back. "Naomi thinks it'd be best if you didn't come up to the hospital, honey. She thinks it might upset Clover."

My mind blinked like a light bulb getting ready to go out. But I heard myself calmly saying, "O.K. Well, I guess that takes care of what to say, huh?" And I heard my forced laughter, as though I'd made a big joke.

"But you can ride in with me. I'd like the company. Look, it's probably for the best, Memphis. It'll give things time to settle down." She was flighty-eyed and starting to babble, talking to fill up the space, maybe even to keep herself from crying. "I'm so glad you're being a big girl about this. It'll work itself out, you'll see." She started around the table, arms out to hug me again, but I couldn't bear it, so I pretended I didn't notice and moved toward the door.

"I'll take my shower first," I said.

She followed right on my heels and stood at the foot of the steps as I raced up them two at a time.

"Memphis! Oh, please don't be hurt. Please." She was still pleading when I closed the bathroom door behind me.

13

Standing at the bathroom window the next morning, looking out across the backyard, I had a hard time believing that only the day before everything had been charged with a nervous electricity and the excruciating tension of waiting. This morning was just as cool and gray, but it was totally different—quiet, almost serene. The vegetable garden showed signs of its neglect. In just three days, weed heads had popped up along the rows, and an air of willfulness had settled in. The chickens were stirring. I needed to feed them. I needed to gather up their eggs. Boss Man, the big Rhode Island Red, flew up atop the henhouse, throwing out his chest, flapping his gorgeous wings, quite sure the new day couldn't start without him. I could hear Aunt Birdie moving around downstairs. The smell of fresh coffee and frying bacon made my stomach gurgle. I'd have to go down and tell her that I wasn't going with her. I didn't want to sit in her car out in the hospital parking lot, feeling less than low.

She called up the stairs. "Hurry along, Memphis."

When I walked into the kitchen barefoot, wearing my favorite old denim shorts, she gave me a surprised look.

"You're not dressed!"

"I don't think I'll go. The chickens. And the garden's looking weedy." I poured myself a glass of milk and spread a piece of toast with peanut butter. I ate quietly and smiled whenever our glances met.

"Did I hurt your feelings last night?"

"I guess. But mostly I don't want to upset anybody anymore ever." That was a lie. I wanted to scream and smash myself against the walls and break dishes. I wanted to get out of Naomi's house and never look back.

Aunt Birdie set her coffee cup down carefully. "I understand. I really do, Memphis."

I shrugged.

"Tell you what, how about we go up to Abbotsville this evening, take in a movie and get a bite to eat? I could use some diversion."

"Sure." I rinsed off the dishes and set them in the drain rack. Naomi's old leather suitcase sat strapped and buckled by the screen door.

Aunt Birdie stood up, smoothing out the wrinkles in her fresh flower-print dress, and I realized she'd gone home earlier and come back. She leaned toward the mirror over the sink and touched up her lipstick with the tip of her little finger, then patted her hair. "That'll have to do," she said to herself. She looped the strap of her purse over one arm and headed for the suitcase. "Hope I remembered everything."

"Want me to carry that out for you?" I moved toward the suitcase, but she picked it up and headed for the door, then hesitated. "Knowing Naomi, she'll probably want a ride back to pick up her car." She glanced around the kitchen. "You might want to straighten things up a bit, just in case."

A small tremor shook my body as I thought of being alone with Naomi.

"Don't forget," Aunt Birdie called back over her shoulder as the screen door slapped shut behind her. "We're going to the movies tonight. I'll pick you up around six. You be ready now!"

I'd just finished vacuuming the living room carpet when I heard the creak of the screen door. My stomach skittered—it was bound to be Naomi, come for her car. I took a deep breath and headed down the hallway.

"Oh," I said, my voice faltering when I saw her. "Aunt Birdie said you were likely to come pick up the Falcon."

She looked thinner, and her face was tight and drawn, as though it was sealed in a veil of wax.

She nodded absently. "Easier to get around," she mumbled. "Where'd I put my keys? Oh, there they are." She swept them up off the kitchen counter. "I'm not staying long, want to get back before Clover wakes up."

I knew I had to say something—something about Clover. But I was so afraid I'd say the wrong thing I simply blurted out, "I'm sorry."

She leaned back against the counter and fiddled with the key ring for a while before she looked up. "I know you're sorry, Memphis. But that doesn't make things right. That doesn't undo the damage."

"But I'm really sorry. . . ."

"What do you want me to say? That everything's just great? Well, it's not. You're self-centered and bullheaded—and frankly, I've just about had enough."

"But . . ."

"I don't want to hear it. It's always Clover's fault, isn't it? Whatever happens, Clover's the demon, right?"

I stared at her in disbelief. She had it all turned around.

"Well, let me tell you something, Memphis. Clover is all she's ever going to be, and I'm all she's got to call her own. You have your whole life ahead of you. If you think for one instant . . . Oh, what's the use?" She shook her head in exasperation.

I knew she was getting ready to leave and stepped in front of her before she could reach the door. The hard, unforgiving edge of her voice had triggered the release of something choked back inside me too long.

"It's not all my fault!" I said, surprised by the loudness of my voice.

She pulled back, startled. "Don't you talk to me like that."

"Don't you talk to me like *that!*" I flung her words back at her.

"What? You stop this right now!"

"No!" I yelled. "You stop it!" I heard my blood rushing through my veins. My eyes burned as though they were on fire, and my body seemed to stretch and grow taller. "You stop saying Rosie isn't my mother! She *is* my mother! She's my mother! I saw her fall on the grass and die! She fell on the grass, and just like that, she was gone! Gone! You've never once asked me how I felt about that! You've never asked me *anything* about her!"

"For God's sake, get hold of yourself!"

"No! You get hold of yourself! You stop telling me everything's my fault—you're to blame, too! You stop calling John Riley a bastard! I didn't ask to be left here! If I knew where he was, I'd crawl to him on my knees if I had to, just to get away from here!" I was screaming now, and I realized I was pounding the sides of my head with my clenched fists.

Naomi's eyes were wide, her mouth open in surprise, but she didn't move away. Instead, she threw down her keys and grabbed my wrists. I was amazed at how strong she was, how easily she forced my hands down. Then I was sobbing, my head drooping down onto her shoulder. She let my storm play itself out before she eased away from me, dampened a dishtowel, and mopped up my wet, burning face.

I dangled helplessly in the flat aftermath of my tantrum while she stood at the sink, her back to me, rinsing out the towel.

"You have to learn to control yourself, Memphis," she said. "This kind of melodrama will get you nowhere."

There wasn't an ounce of anything left in me—not anger, not rage, not even self-pity. The only thing my blank mind could comprehend was that my grandmother and I would never understand each other. I slid down onto a chair and buried my face against my arms.

I heard her say, "I have to get back to the hospital." Then she sighed and said, "I don't want Clover coming home to this kind of . . ." I looked up as her words faded. She glanced back at me with the saddest face I'd ever seen.

"Rosie broke my heart," she said. Then she picked up her car keys and left.

Once Naomi was gone, I took a long, hot shower, trying to scrub off the hurt. I was upstairs in my room, pulling a comb through my wet, tangled hair, when Samson's bicycle bell rang three times out in the front yard. I eased to the window and stood out of sight behind the thin curtain. I didn't know how I'd ever be able to talk to him or even look at him again without thinking of that kiss. Watching him now, my body felt strange, unfamiliar, as though the brush of a feather could send me jumping out of my skin. He waited for a long time, then walked his bike back across the yard, hopped on, and sailed down Blue Parrot Road toward town.

Good-bye, Samson. And good-bye, Blue Parrot, too. I was leaving. I'd made up my mind. I didn't know when or how, just that I would go. I didn't belong here. I'd never belong here. I looked tenderly at my trolls lined up in front of the dresser mirror. *We want to go with you,* they seemed to say. So yes, I'd take my trolls. I picked up Lady Althea's raggedy little bag of pungent magic, cupped it to my nose, and inhaled deeply. *I'll have to go with you too,* it whispered, *to keep you safe.* Who knows how much worse things could have gotten without it?

Aunt Birdie picked me up at six on the dot. I'd tried to make myself look as pretty as she liked to tell me I was, wearing a white wraparound skirt and an aqua linen shirt I'd made from one of her old Simplicity patterns.

"I love that color on you," she said, and I relaxed.

We saw *Butch Cassidy and the Sundance Kid*. Aunt Birdie said, "What a treat, and it only took three years to get to Abbotsville," and, "Where was Robert Redford when I was growing up?" She acted younger, smiling at everybody and joking around. She even gave the theater manager a flirty little smile as we were leaving. He said, "Come back again, ladies."

Aunt Birdie said, "We might just do that," and nudged me in the ribs.

Afterward we stopped at JoAnne's, a fancy drive-in at the edge of town, and got chocolate milkshakes and big, juicy hamburgers with all the trimmings.

It was a little after nine-thirty as we headed down the highway back to Blue Parrot. Lights were flicking on in the small houses along the road, the families inside settled down for the evening in front of their television sets. But every once in a while, I saw someone out on a porch or walking by a window inside, and I stared till we were past as though they might let me in on a secret.

Cars coming from the other direction began popping on their headlights, and the sudden beams on the road made the growing night seem darker.

"I better turn my lights on so I can see where I'm going," Aunt Birdie said with a little laugh.

I hadn't mentioned Clover all evening, hadn't told her about seeing Naomi earlier. I cleared my throat.

"How's Clover?" I asked.

"Oh, she's better today. She'll probably be coming home next week."

It was the opening she'd been waiting for. She began talking in a rush—something about things having to change, everybody having to do some hard thinking—but I wasn't really listening. My satisfied stomach and the steady hum of the Buick's engine had lulled me into a reverie. Maybe I could get a job like the waitress back at the drive-in, meet people who would like me just the way I was.

"What?" She glanced over at me.

"Huh?"

"You were mumbling. You're not thinking of doing something stupid, are you?"

"No," I said wearily. "I was just thinking maybe I could get a job after school, like at JoAnne's. Get out of the house more." I leaned my head back and closed my eyes.

We drove on in silence. Then Aunt Birdie turned on the car radio, and the soft strains of "When My Blue Moon Turns to Gold Again" drifted out. I could hear her fingertips tapping lightly against the steering wheel.

"Have you given much thought to what you want out of life, honey? What you want to do with yourself?"

It seemed a curious question, and I felt vaguely uncomfortable. I wanted what I'd always wanted—to hear the old VW chugging up the driveway, to hear the banging on the front door, to hear John Riley say, *I've come for my daughter.*

Instead I said, "Be happy, I guess."

She reached over and patted my arm. "Why don't you stay with me for a while until things settle down?"

A pinpoint of light flared at the back of my tired mind—she and Naomi had probably talked. But that was O.K. At least she was offering me a resting place where I could figure out what to do, which way to go. I leaned into her soft voice. She was talking about her cousin, Velma, in Florida, how she might go down for a visit in August, how she'd love for me to go with her. My head nestled against her shoulder, and I floated into the luminous embrace of sleep, where I skimmed along a sparkling white beach, free as a seabird. In the background, Aunt Birdie waved from the balcony of a pink apartment building set against a brilliant blue sky.

14

June 1975

I never went back to Naomi's. As the weeks passed, Aunt Birdie and I fell into a comfortable routine. Being in that sprawling, welcoming house with her and marmalade Fannie seemed, as she put it, righter than rain. Oh, she didn't take a nickel's worth of junk off me, but she gave me elbow room to come to a reckoning with myself.

It's funny how Naomi and I just seem to have this unspoken agreement that we're all better off now. She tries in her way to be friendly sometimes, but there's a distance between us, and I doubt that's ever going to change. Being born into a family doesn't necessarily mean they'll all love you, I guess.

Looking back, I feel as though I survived an earthquake. When those three days had ended, nothing was, or ever would be, the same. I left my childhood behind with a great wrenching good-bye. Even Samson's sweet cinnamon kiss, I realize now, was a tender farewell to the children we had outgrown.

He spent the rest of that summer up in New Jersey with his grandparents. When fall came, he didn't return.

He goes to a boys' school up there. He writes once in a while, says he belongs to a science club and is running track. He says he likes New Jersey, but the winters are long and cold, and he misses prowling through Blue Parrot's wild pine woods. I answer, telling him about the goings-on at Oaklee High and the interesting people I meet at my after-school job as gofer at the *Oaklee Tribune*. After my last letter, he wrote back and said I was surely going to be a big-time reporter someday. I was puffed up with myself for a week! Mrs. Greeley showed me a picture of him last month, and I hardly recognized him—it's been two years. He's grown tall and looks almost like a movie star. When she told me he'd be coming home for the summer, my stomach did a flip-flop.

Life in Blue Parrot goes on. Mrs. Preacher Dalton finally got to be somebody's mother. She has twin boys, Ethan and Joshua. When she sent out Christmas cards last year, there was a picture of her fat, year-old baby boys on the front, and underneath she'd written, *Praise God for Answered Prayers!* Aunt Birdie chuckled and said to stay tuned!

Sometimes I see Clover passing by. She wears a straw cowboy hat with a splay of turkey feathers fanning back to one side. I left it on her front porch last November for her birthday. Nobody knows I did that, not even Aunt Birdie, and somehow that makes me feel good.

Lately, I've kind of studied my life with a steadier eye. I think about John Riley and how he walked away from me and, as far as I know, never looked back. Maybe deep down inside I've been way past angry with him for years—and maybe I took it out on Clover.

She finally understands that I won't be coming back to live in her house, that I've made Aunt Birdie my new mama. She's even started waving. Last week she walked up our driveway to the porch and showed me this perfect little opaline beetle that she held cupped in her hands.

"So pretty," she said in her strange, misshapen words.

"Yes," I said. "So pretty."

I'm beginning to understand that life just rolls along without any hard feelings toward anyone and that what you decide to do about things is its rudder. As some old geezer said on TV the other day, you buys your ticket and you takes your ride. Aunt Birdie said, "Give that man a twenty-five-cent cigar!" Her way of agreeing with him. Yes, life is sure enough tough. But sometimes, if you're lucky, there's a rainbow thread or two running through it—like Aunt Birdie. Like Samson.

Lately Aunt Birdie has started talking more about Rosie, about what a beautiful and funny girl she was. I came home from school this past Valentine's Day, and there on my dresser was a framed snapshot of Rosie when she was about fifteen, same age as I am now. It's comforting.

When Aunt Birdie came home from Naomi's last Friday with Rosie's cremation urn, she said, "Little by little, we'll put it all to rest."

We buried Rosie's ashes Sunday afternoon, along with the mangled guitar, in the shade of the chinaberry tree in the backyard. Naomi didn't come, said she didn't want Clover getting upset. More likely she's the one to worry about. I wonder if she'll ever make her peace with Rosie. Anyway, we planted a cherish rose bush there, and I think my Rosie Mama's spirit finally felt free to lift up and make its way back to wherever it is we all come from.

After Sheriff Wilson left—he's been showing up for Sunday dinners pretty regularly—Aunt Birdie and I walked out to the far edge of the pecan grove to watch the sunset. Coming back to the house, she looped her arm through mine and said carefully, "John Riley may never come back, you know. Someday you might have to let go of that notion."

I nodded, for it seems every day that I live in Aunt Birdie's house, I grow more and more into my own life and all it holds for me. I'm coming to understand that home isn't brick or board. It's a feeling of belonging, of being at peace right where you are. I know now I may never set eyes on John Riley again. But my stubborn heart believes his curiosity will get the best of him. I think he'll want to know how I turn out.

If I should look up one day and see him walking toward me, even if I'm grown and married with children of my own, I'm not going to think about all the years I waited for him. I'm not going to say one word about heartache or broken promises. I'm going to open my arms wide. And I'm going to say, "Welcome home, Daddy."